Lock Down Publications and Ca$h
Presents

CONFESSIONS OF A DOPEBOY
Diary Of A Hustler

Written By
NICHOLAS LOCK

Copyright © 2024 NICHOLAS LOCK
CONFESSIONS OF A DOPEBOY

All rights reserved. No part of this book may be reproduced in any form or by electronic or mechanical means, including information storage and retrieval systems without permission in writing from the publisher, except by a reviewer who may quote brief passages in review.

First Edition 2024

Printed in the United States of America

This is a work of fiction. Names, characters, places, and incidents either are products of the author's imagination or are used fictitiously. Any similarity to actual events or locales or persons, living or dead, is entirely coincidental.

Lock Down Publications
P.O. Box 944
Stockbridge, GA 30281
www.lockdownpublications.com

Like our page on Facebook: Lock Down Publications
www.facebook.com/lockdownpublications.ldp

Stay Connected with Us!

Text **LOCKDOWN** to 22828 to stay up-to-date with new releases, sneak peaks, contests and more…

Like our page on Facebook:
Lock Down Publications

Join Lock Down Publications/The New Era Reading Group

Visit our website:
www.lockdownpublications.com

Follow us on Instagram:
Lock Down Publications

Email Us: We want to hear from you!

Shout-Outs

I have to thank God for this ability to play with words and for giving me this crazy imagination.

Ca$h and the LDP Staff- thanks for the opportunity to allow the world to get a glimpse of the many different stories I have to tell.

To The Fans- Thank you for all the support; without y'all, this wouldn't be possible. And to all the women who keep asking me when I'm gonna write a book for the ladies. I got y'all. When this series concludes, that'll be my next project! Be on the lookout.

This is book #9, so hopefully, I've shouted you out already but if I forgot. My bad! It ain't over, so I'll get to you. To the fans who want to give me their feedback and critiques, you can contact me on Facebook: Nicholas Lock

PROLOGUE

"Snatch, something doesn't seem right," Demon said glancing around. They had just pulled up to Demon's house and Snatch was about to drop him off and he was going to head home; tomorrow was going to be a big day.

"What is it Brody?" Snatch question reaching for his stick.

"I don't know; something just seems kind of off." Demon cocked his XD .40 and got out.

Snatch got out with Demon, his pistol down by his side. The full moon was giving off just enough light that the night wasn't pitch black. Snatch now felt what Demon was feeling. Everything was eerily quiet; the crickets weren't even chirping. Snatch shivered and got goosebumps. Snatch and Demon looked around one last time before entering the house. Demon cut the lights on in the house and they went through the house room by room making sure everything was to the good and nobody was in hiding.

"Yous'a scary ass, pussy ass nigga," Snatch pushed Demon. "Something doesn't seem right" he mocked Demon.

"Whateva, motherfucka. You better take your ass home before the wifey do something to your ass. You know you're supposed to be home before streetlights come on, Demon gave it back. "What? Nigga, I'm the king of my castle," Snatch bragged opening the door.

Whap! Whap! Something hard hit Snatch twice in the face causing him to stumble backwards into Demon. Demon caught Snatch and they both fell to the carpet.

"Surprise! You motherfuckers thought that shit was sweet but now it's time to pay the piper. Well, Snatch, you're going to pay the piper but you Mr. Demon, you're about to pay the devil a visit," he pointed his gun at Demon and squeezed the trigger. Boom! Boom! Boom! "Now you have to bury your mans."

Chapter 1

"I be in the loop; she be in a group. Brody wants her friend, throw an alley-hoop," Lil Babys hit blasted out of the speakers in Club Halo.

"How can I lose when we the who who's," Snatch rapped along with Lil Baby.

Snatch and his day-one nigga Demon had just graduated from high school and were celebrating along with about fifty other seniors.

"Buy me a drink," Sasha walked up and asked Snatch.

"I ain't the trickin' type, you in the wrong section," he shot back continuing to bob his head to the music.

"Stop play nigga, damn!" She continued

Sasha was so used to getting what she wanted from niggas that Snatch turning her down was crushing her self-esteem. Sasha was a true head-turner. Sasha was a freshman at Fayetteville State University. She had smooth chocolate skin, pretty brown eyes, long lashes, full sensuous lips and a body to die for. Her hair was always done in the latest fashions. At the moment, she had on a 36-inch red weave.

Sasha knew Snatch was a hustler just by the clothes he had on because he was too young to have a high-end career. Snatch was sporting a pair of black Amiri jeans, a black Amiri button up and some black retro 7's. His three-inch-thick Cuban link and small Rolex were the only jewelry he wore.

Snatch would've loved nothing more than to buy Sasha a drink but if he spent some more money, he was going to fuck up his re-up. Snatch looked the part of a big-time dope boy but him and Demon were really just small timers.

"Fuck school! I'm glad we're finally done with that shit," Demon said in his raspy voice, dapping Snatch up.

"Me too," Snatch agreed looking at the fifty-dollar bill Demon had slid him on the sneak tip. Snatch looked at Demon like what's this for, and he cut his eyes at Sasha,

"Whatchu drinking?" Snatch asked her.

"Peach Cîroc," she smiled running her hands over the waves in Snatch's head.

Snatch ordered her a shot and put his back to the bar. Just about every woman that passed by would double-take at Snatch and Demon.

Both were easy on the eyes. Snatch was 6'0, red light-skinned, freckles, reddish-orange hair, grey piercing eyes, on athletic build and the only facial hair he had on his face was a mustache.

Demon was also 6'0 but he had rich, dark chocolate skin, hazel eyes, a stocky build and ten wicks that hung just below his shoulders. Demon was the more aggressive one of the two. Snatch was passive-aggressive.

Demon would go from zero to a hundred in two seconds. And he was notorious for going above and beyond. Demon earned his name because he was downright demonic when it was go time. Snatch wasn't a slouch in the getting active department; he just wasn't as quick to snap out like Demon.

He tended to let it build up then he would explode. But when he did explode, there wasn't only talking to him, all he wanted to do was shed blood.. Snatch's mother nicknamed him Snatch because when he was a baby, he would always snatch things away from people. Snatch told people he got the name because he was known for snatching niggas girls.

"What's your number?" Sasha asked. Snatch didn't say anything; he just grabbed her phone and put his number in.

"I'ma check you out later," he dismissed her. Sasha walked off in search of her homegirls while Snatch continued to look in the crowd.

"Did you get the number nigga?" Demon asked.

"Of course. You act like my name ain't big Snatch or something!" Snatch bragged,

"Demon, who is old girl in the yellow shorts over there?" he pointed to a petite chocolate beauty. He asked Demon because he got out more than he did.

"That's Asa. She is older than us, she is like twenty-seven or something like that. Why you digging that?"

"I don't know yet," Snatch locked eyes with Asa and motioned for her to come over. She walked over to Snatch and Demon but she brought her homegirls with her.

"What up?" she stood in front of Snatch and popped her lips back.

"I can't really call it sexy. How are you doing?" Snatch flashed his pearly whites.

"I'm fine, thank you for asking." She looked over at her homegirls.

"Fine isn't the word, beautiful would be a more accurate description," he said causing her to blush.

"Oh, he one of them smooth talkin' ass red niggas," one of her homegirls chimed in.

"Is it still smooth talking if I'm telling the truth?" Snatch shot back.

"Damn, how y'all fine ladies doing tonight? Whateva they are drinkin' is on me!" Chance walked up and yelled at the bartender.

"Patron!" one of the girls said.

"How old are you?" Asa asked Snatch.

"Eighteen, this is our graduation party for the most part."

"Damn Asa, you trying to rob the cradle ain't you? I done told you I'm ready to settle down with you," Chance shot his shot.

"My nigga, she good. Go find you anotha chick to holla at," Snatch told him.

"Mann, if you don't shut your broke ass up! Stay in your lane lil nigga before I put you there," he warned.

"Broke? Put me there then pussy," Snatch smiled looking over at Demon who was mugging Chance.

"Yea *broke*! Nigga, you only copping two ounces and you and ya mans be bustin them down so y'all only getting an ounce apiece," Chance put them on blast and the girls started laughing. That set Snatch off! He was going to let it go because words didn't move him but the women laughing chipped at his ego.

The ego was the cause of many murders. But before Snatch could make his move, Demon slipped by him and hit Chance with a two-piece that knocked him out cold. They started stomping him out then his homeboys saw what was going on and rushed over causing a melee. Snatch was fighting three dudes at one time trying to hold his own when Action jumped in and stumbled over one of the dudes. Snatch picked one of the dudes up and slammed him and went to help Action. Snatch punched the dude Action was going toe to toe within the kidneys sending him to his knees.

Action gave him a knee to the face knocking his teeth across the dance floor. The bouncers started spraying mace putting an end to the brawl. Snatch and Demon got to Demon's black Cadillac XTS and were pulling off when they saw Action sprinting through the parking lot.

"Get in." Snatch rolled his window down. Action got in, took her long blond hair out of the bun and let it fall.

"Roll up, my motherfuckin' heart hurts," she said sprawling across the backseat out of breath.

"You the craziest white girl I know," Snatch said rolling up the blunt of white runts. Action's real name was Meredith but Snatch had given her the name Action because she was about that action. They'd met in middle school at Ramsey

Street Alternative School and that's when he saw that she was about that drama.

Ramsey Street Alternative was where you got sent to when the school you're attending didn't want to deal with you anymore. It's usually after you've been suspended three times. Every other day, she was putting her hands on somebody, and it didn't matter if it was a man or a woman, she could care less.

And what fooled most people was that she looked like a girly girl. Action had long blond hair, blue eyes, pointed nose, Kylie Jenner lips and was petite with a heart-shaped butt.

Her C-cups sat up high and firm. At 5'9, she was taller than the average girl which was probably why Snatch had never seen her lose a one-on-one fight. She was always around Snatch and Demon. If you saw one, there was a good chance the other one was somewhere in the vicinity. Action was eighteen just like Snatch and Demon. She was from the project called Colony Place off Owen Drive. Snatch and Demon stayed in Holiday Park, a neighborhood connected to Colony Place.

There were only two roads leading in and out. When you first turn off Owen Drive, you are in Holiday Park. Depending on which road you took, it would take you from Holiday Park to Holland Homes Apartments to Colony Place or from Holiday Park sat at the very back down in a hole. There were seven two-story buildings that made up Colony Place.

"Are you going to pass the blunt or not?" she tried snatching it from Snatch.

"I had to get my puffs in because y'all two be chiefin' like hell." He passed her the blunt "Watch out! There goes Chance!" Demon yelled.

Boc! Boc! Boc! Boc!

Chapter 2

The windows to Demon's XTS shattered as Chance and one of his homeboys fired out the window of his red Navigator. Action grabbed the ARP off the backseat and let it talk shit. LAT! LAT! LAT!LAT! she sent rounds of death across the front of the Navigators grill and it started smoking and cut off. Demon sped away from the scene.

"Yo fuck that! Where that nigga be at?" Demon asked ready to spin.

"He one of them Murk Mob Niggas. He be over there off the Murch on Jasper Street," Snatch informed him.

"What are y'all trying to do?" Action was ready to get active.

"Fuck that! Swing through there" Snatch put one in the head of his Smith and Wesson .45.

Snatch had never really put in any major work when it came to busting his gun. All he'd done was put a few holes in some clouds. He was given to fight than he was to shoot. Snatch would rather get money and fuck bitches than to get involved in some drama. But the tequila running through his system coupled with his adrenaline had him ready to drop something.

Nardo Wicks who wanted some blared out the alpines as Demon drove to Chance's side of the town. Chance must've called ahead and told his people what happened because when Demon got to the intersection of Jasper and Murchison Road, niggas started busting!

The Cadillac started taking rounds from all sides, it was all Demon could do to get them back to their side of town without any of them getting hit. We ain't going out like that! We ain't got no choice but to spin back. We gon' let it die down and then we gon' strike. Action said before getting out the car and going into the building. Demon and Snatch both nodded their heads and went home with murder on their minds.

****

"Get up off yo ass and clean this nasty ass room!" Snatch's mother yelled and snatched the covers off him.

"Chill ma," he said groggily.

"Well, get your ass up. You need to be finding out what you're going to do with your life now that you're done with school."

Snatch sat up, rubbed the sleep out of his eyes and looked at his alarm clock.

"Ma, it's 7:30 in the morning, I'll do it when I wake up." He pulled the covers back over his head.

"Sumayee Kareen Brooks! You got five seconds to get your ass up or it's gonna be me and you," her voice went from high to low.

Snatch knew her voice did that when she was on the verge of getting mad, so he sat up. He knew how far to push her. Snatch didn't necessarily fear his mother, but he respected her and her anger. His mother was a 5'9, 170 pounds, light brown-skinned fireball. Mia was what everyone called her and was still in the top ten of the baddest women in Fayetteville, North Carolina.

Both of her children had inherited her grey eyes. At thirty-four, her 36' B's, 24-inch waist and 40-inch ass were still top-notch with no flab. She was thicker than a cold bowl of grits! Her pretty face had fooled many women and men into thinking shit was sweet until she went off, but by then, it was too late. When she saw that Snatch was up, she went down the hall to his sister Alayna's room.

"Layna, we're going to see your dad today but if you're not ready by the time I'm ready, you'll be a left ass." She went into her room and closed the door not waiting to see if Alayna had gotten up.

Alayna was Snatch's sixteen-year-old sister and the cause of many of his headaches. Alayna had already developed their mother's physique and attitude. Snatch and Demon stayed putting their hands on a nigga behind her grown ass.

Alayna was 5'5 red like their father, with grey eyes and a body just like their mom's. The thing with Alayna was that she was fast but she wasn't fast to the point of having sex. She just entertained boys all the time and Snatch hated it. She always told Snatch she was just talking to the boys and that was it because Snatch had given her the game.

So, she knew all the tricks and sayings that boys used to try and get her to have sex. Snatch walked by Alayna's room and saw her scrambling around looking for something to wear. She stopped when she saw Snatch in her doorway.

"Are you coming with us this time?' she inquired. Snatch stood there looking at her with a blank stare because he knew that she already knew the answer to her own question. Snatch hadn't gone to see their dad since he was eleven years old. Their dad Quiet Storm who everyone called Storm for short was a hustler's hustler.

He got the name Quiet Storm because that's exactly what he was, a quiet storm. He was a silent killer but more than that was the plug! Storm had the best heroin on the East Coast. He supplied every state between Maryland and Florida. Everyone he dealt with loved him because he showed so much love. Storm had out a lot of niggas on their feet.

The Rico act got him a life sentence in the Feds and he hadn't got caught with a single piece of dope. The Feds took every penny he had, all his property and cars. His right-hand man Jake had got caught with forty kilos of uncut heroin and gave up Storm.

They tried to get Storm to give up his connect for a ten-year bid but he refused earning himself a life sentence. His man Jake got a five-year bid. Jake got stabbed to death in his first year in the yard while in the shower. Snatch used to make it his duty to go with his mom and sister to see Pops but when he turned eleven, all of that came to an end. He could remember like it was yesterday…..

They were all in the visitation room at Big Sandy in Kentucky and his mom was shedding tears as usual. Snatch had a good understanding of why his dad was never coming home but he still had the mind of a little boy. Their dad was in the process of trying to calm their mom down when things got out of hand.

"Dad, do you want to come home?" Snatch questioned.

"Of course, I do" Storm had a puzzled look on his face.

"Well, why didn't you tell and come home?" he asked naively.

Snatch had been at one of his friends' houses and overheard a conversation in which his friend's dad said if Storm woulda given up the connect, he would have been home in eight years.

"For one, you better watch your fucking mouth. And secondly, I'm a gangsta with morals, principles and integrity. You don't do the crime if you can't do the time. A rat is the scum of the earth! A rat would rather take you away from your family and loved ones because they can't handle the consequences of their actions," he said gritting his teeth and leaning into Snatch's face.

"You listen and you listen good. You're a gangsta's son, so you have a gangsta blood running through your veins. We never fold, we're leaders, not followers. We stand ten toes down no matter the consequences and we man up. Not only was your daddy a gangsta but your mother was as well. So, you were born to be a real nigga. Under no circumstances are you to tell on your potna. And make that your last time you ever question my actions."

"Whatever," Snatch mumbled.

SLAP! Storm slapped Snatch out of the chair. The C. O.'s didn't say a word. Storm might've been off the streets, but his reputation reached coast to coast. It was known that Storm would get you killed quick. He had lost his money, but he still had a lot of power and respect. His plug had made sure of that when he kept it solid and didn't tell on him.

Snatch got back in the chair and didn't say another word until he got in the car.

"I'm never going to see him again," he told his mother

"You know I'm not, so stop playin'," he said.

"You need to get over that shit and let it go. That's our dad and it's a possibility he'll never get out. Our visits are one of the only ways to escape those walls," Alayna said and Snatch walked into the bathroom.

He wasn't about to have a conversation about a nigga he didn't fuck with like that. He washed his face, brushed his teeth, went back to his room and called Janice.

"Boy, do you know what time it is?" she answered on the third ring.

"My mom and them about to go see my dad, so you need to be making your way over here when they leave."

"Okay," she said, and he hung up.

Ten minutes later, Snatch's mom and sister left. Then thirty seconds later, Janice knocked on the door.

"Took you long enough." Snatch slapped her on the ass as she walked by him.

Snatch followed her down the hall to his room; the whole time, he was looking in on her ass as it wobbled in the black leggings she had on.

"You didn't call me in two days but the minute you call and tell me to come over, my stupid ass come over." She sat on the edge of the bed and pouted, looking sexy as fuck.

Snatch and Janice weren't a couple in an official sense, but they carried out all the acts that couples do, including the fighting and arguing. Snatch and Janice had met in the eighth grade and had been a couple in the beginning, but once they got to high school, things changed.

Snatch's good looks made him one of the schools most wanted. So girls were throwing themselves at him creating a rift between him and Janice. They stopped talking for six months but then Janice, her mom and brother moved to the house across the street from Snatch. But just like Snatch, Janice was a head-turner.

Janice was 5'6, had smooth dark brown skin, silky black shoulder length hair and doe-shaped light brown eyes. She had B cups but made up for it with her thick thighs and fat ass. Janice was built like Ghetto Barbie. Her full lips were Snatch's favorite feature.

"You're exactly tight, it's been two days, so you know I'm backed up. We'll talk about all that otha shit in a lil bit." Snatch stripped naked and walked over to her.

"You make me sick." She grabbed his swollen dick and sucked the head into her warm mouth.

Snatch grabbed a handful of her hair and began to guide her head down back and forth,

"Quit playing and suck this dick," Snatch complained, looking down at her.

Snatch backed up and told her to get up. Janice stood up, looking Snatch in the eyes. He grabbed the sweater she had on and pulled it over her head, exposing her perky B cups. Snatch caressed one of her nipples, making it stand out an inch.

"Take them leggings off," he whispered in a voice filled with lust.

Janice turned around and started tugging the leggings down. Once she got them over her butt, she bent straight over and began tugging them down her legs slowly. Janice's wet pussy poked out from between her legs making Snatch's pole get harder.

"Mmmm," she moaned as he rubbed the head of his wood up and down her center, coating it with her juices.

"Now get nasty for daddy," Snatch said huskily.

Janice got down on her knees and went in! She grabbed the base of Snatch's pole and took him to the back of her throat. Janice started throwing her head back and forth in a circular motion taking Snatch in and out of her mouth at a rapid pace.

"That's right! Suck daddy dick!" His eyes rolled in the back of his head.

Janice rubbed her clit in circles continuing to bob back and forth on his pole. Snatch's nut felt like it came from the bottom of his feet. He clutched her hair at the root and his lips locked up as he released his kids in her mouth. Janice swallows without having to be told. She knew what and how Snatch liked his sex. Snatch pushed her onto her back and crawled between her legs.

"Tell me how you want it?"

"Hard and fast," she replied.

Snatch put Janice's legs on his shoulders and looked down, admiring her sex. Her pussy was hairless fat and wet. Janice's love petals opened revealing her clit. If he ate pussy, he would've dove in tongue first but that wasn't his thing. Snatch entered Janice making her arch her back up off the back. Snatch pushed all the way in until their pelvis touched causing Janice's moan to get caught in her throat. Snatch started driving into Janice just how she asked, hard and fast.

"Yesss baby! Fuck me good!" she moaned raking her hands down his stomach.

Janice was making a puddle on the floor. Every time would push in and out Janice's pussy was making a slurping noise.

"Damn this pussy good." Snatch gritted his teeth.

Snatch put his hands on the bottom of her things for leverage and sped up. SMACK! SMACK! SMACK! Their flesh sapping together, and moans were the only sounds in the room.

"Here it comes baby, here it comes," Janice whispered.

"Uhnnn!" she came all over Snatch's pole making the puddle on the floor bigger.

Snatch stroked a few more times and collapsed on top of her coating Janice's insides with semen. They got in the bed and fell asleep in the spoon position.

Chapter 3

"Don't play with me nigga. If I don't hear from you tonight, I'ma post that video of you eating my pussy on Facebook," Janice threatened as Snatch walked her across the street to her house.

"You post that and I'ma post me bustin' in your mouth and you swallowin' it" he said palming her butt. "Now go ahead and try me."

"Just call me" she disappeared in her house.

Snatch walked down the road to Colony Place. As soon as he went down the hill and bent the corner, he saw Demon on the basketball court playing a four-on-four game. It seemed like everyone in the projects was out. The hood was jumping! The sun was in the middle of the sky without a cloud in sight making 85 feel like it was 100. Snatch was complaining because the heat had the women out in droves, and they had on next to nothing.

Everywhere you looked, you saw booty shorts, skirts and skimpy tops. Some even had on bathing suits. Someone had opened the fire hydrant and all the kids were running through the water having a good time. There was even a nigga cooking on the grill selling plates. Snatch looked and saw Action sitting on one of the green boxes and walked over to her.

"What it is, what it ain't?" Snatch grabbed a seat beside her.

"What it is blunt of alien O.G." she pulled out a bag of weed. "What it ain't is this hot ass weather." Action tugged on her shirt.

Action had on a pair of white boy shorts that hugged her curves just right. The shirt she was wearing was cut in half showing off the fact that she didn't own a stomach.

"Eat!" Snatch yelled as Demon drove to the basket and dunked on a dude.

"Snatch, you straight?" A customer walked up.

"Always."

"Let me get two dubs then."

Snatch served him and cuffed the money.

"Boy, you better not!" Action yelled

Snatch turned to see Rambo pointing a super soaker water gun at her. Rambo was twelve going on twenty-one and bad as hell! And he had a bunch of little boys he ran with that were just like him.

"Give me ten dollars or a bag of weed and I'll let you live," he said with a straight face.

"I ain't giving yo lil ass—" was all she got out and he squeezed the trigger spraying her then took off running.

Snatch busted out laughing because Action was mad as hell and it was all over her face. She was red as hell!

"Girl, it ain't nothing but…oh hell nah." Snatch looked down at his blue Polo shorts. "What the fuck is he spraying Clorox?"

"Yea, that's bleach!" Action smelled her hands.

Snatch took off after Rambo, he was gonna whoop his ass!

"Beat his ass!" Rambo's mom Tiffany yelled watching him run past.

Snatch caught Rambo and pushed him to the ground.

"This is $300 shorts you fucked up, boy." Snatch removed his belt and Rambo sprayed him again, this really pissed him off.

Snatch drew back the belt and then Demon yelled, "Get down! Get down!"

Snatch looked over his should and saw two cars full of Murk niggas hanging out the windows.

"Yeeaa!" Chance screamed and aimed his Draco at Snatch.

KAH! KAH! KAH! Dirt kicked up around Snatch's feet.

Snatch sprinted toward the building where Action was shooting twin 40's. Snatch could hear the bullets whizzing past his head as he ran. He could feel death breathing on the back of his neck. He made it to the building and dove in the breezeway. Snatch had never been scared in his life. He swore to himself right then that he'd never get caught without his gun again. The shooting stopped and he walked out of the breezeway.

"Nooo! No! No!" A woman screamed at the top of her lungs.

Snatch looked and saw a woman cradling a little girl in her arms. He looked closer and saw that the bottom half of her face was gone. All Snatch could do was shake his head. He knew that it was officially war now and there would never be peace again between the two sides.

"Where you get all these guns from?" Snatch questioned Demon.

Snatch, Demon and Action were at a friend's apartment in Colony Place that they stashed shit at and trapped out of. They were in the living room where Demon had about twenty guns on the table. Action had a p90 assault rifle laid across her lap, Demon had two mini-14's and Snatch grabbed a Heckler and Kach MP10 submachine gun. No handguns were allowed on this trip.

"We about to spin on every block them Murk Mob niggas be on. If they out there, squeeze, ain't no such thing as innocent bystanders" Demon said looking down the barrel of one of the mini 14's.

They filed out of the apartment and were making their way to a stolen Trackhawk when Rambo's bad ass popped up out of nowhere.

"Rambo, that's one of the feists' ways to get shot!" Action chastised him.

"I'm comin' with y'all," he said.

"Boy, if you don't take yo bad ass in the house," she said.

"No, I'm trying to spin and I got my own gun" Ramon produced a baby .40." That was my little cousin that got killed earlier. So either you can take me with you or I'ma ride my bike over there. Either way, I'ma spin" he looked them all in the eyes.

Snatch looked Rambo in the eyes, and he didn't see a twelve-year-old little boy anymore; he saw a killer in the making. His eyes held no emotion. It was crazy how the hood worked because circumstances were turning twelve-year-old Rambo and eighteen-year-old Snatch into cold-hearted killers.

"If you freeze up yo ass, find yourself on the Murk behind enemy lines," Snatch said.

"You can't be serious," Action protested.

"He good," Demon agreed handing Rambo one of the mini 14's.

She shook her head and got in the driver's seat. Demon and Snatch both climbed in the back and Rambo got in the front. Rambo bobbed his head to Lil Durk as they drove through Massey Hill. Snatch shook off the shivers as they drove past the country jail.

Everybody cocked their guns when they turned off the boulevard onto Filter Plant Road and came out beside bronco square. Action made the left onto Murchison Road which everyone calls the Murk for short and started creeping. She turned into Elliot Circle and slowed down.

They got to the back and saw about ten dudes standing around. Rambo didn't waste any time, as soon as he saw them, he came out the window with the mini 14. TAT! TAT!

TAT! Rambo let his assault rifle get some get back for his cousin. Two of the dudes fell and Rambo really turned up.

"Don't run now nigga!" he yelled, getting up on the window sill.

Of the ten dudes standing around, Rambo put bullets in seven of them.

"Action, pull over and put these niggas out because it looked like they froze up to me," he told her getting back in the jeep.

"Nigga, you jumped the gun but we about to show you how to put that real work in," Snatch shot back. Action pulled out of Elliott Circle and made a left. They pulled up to the light and saw about twenty dudes and ten women in the Suburban parking lot.

Demon came out the window letting the mini 14 talk. Snatch got out and came around the jeep with the MP10. LA! LA! LA! LA! The dudes in the small parking lot were scrambling everywhere trying to dodge the pain the submachine guns were sending at them.

Snatch glanced back and saw Action on the hood of the jeep with the P90 assault rifle jumping in her hands bringing a smile to his face. The oncoming sirens forced them back to the jeep. When the smoke cleared, there were ten dead and three in critical condition. They went back to the hood up one on Chance and the Murk Mob.

Chapter 4

"Snatch, it's about that time, I only got two grams left," Demon said.

"Yea, you right because I'm down to my last three. I'ma call J and tell him wassup." Snatch grabbed his phone.

J was the guy they copped their work from every week. He had a trap off Ireland Drive on Sterling Street that did numbers. J didn't answer the first two times but Snatch needed to re-up so he kept hitting him.

"Snatch, it's over for you, I can't serve you my dog. Chance is cutting your water off," J finally answered.

"Damn, that nigga your daddy or something?" Snatch screwed his face up.

"First off, watch your tongue, that's who I get my work from. So, what you want me to do, take food out of my family's mouth just to serve you? It ain't happenin," he said and hung up.

Snatch looked at the phone. He didn't respect J's move but at the same time, he understood it.

"We gotta dead this nigga Chance!" Snatch punched his hand. "He got to J and he not gon serves us; no more talking about Chance is cutting our water off."

"Fuck J. He ain't the only nigga in the city with work. You can't keep real nigga down forever, we gonin' be straight," Demon said with confidence.

They both got on their phones calling around trying to get someone to serve them but everybody they called wouldn't fuck with them. They were getting a world-class lesson in war. It cost money to go to war and Chance was fucking their money up putting them behind the curve. They were learning that you don't go to war with someone who has more power and influence than you.

But what Chance wasn't taking into consideration was that overall, Snatch, Demon and Action didn't give two fucks about it. They weren't used to having shit! So, when they didn't have shit, it wasn't anything new. They were willing to risk it all just to dead Chance. Chance was giving out the lesson right now but if Snatch had something to say about it, he would be the teacher before long.

"Fuck it bra, we'll figure something out. I gotta go take Layna to get her nails done. We'll put a game plan together later." Snatch dapped Demon up and headed out.

Snatch hopped the fence in Demon's backyard and came out on his street. When he walked in the house, Alyna was already ready.

"Dang boy! You gon' make me miss my appointment," she said.

"Shut up! You act like it's not your homegirl that's doing your nails. And go ahead and change them shorts because they're too little and too tight," Snatch said and walked down the hall to his room.

Alayna was wearing some purple cootchie cutters, a tight white tank top with the words Queen in purple letters across the front and some white and purple Jordan fours.

Snatch walked down the hall to his room, grabbed his gun and put it on his hip. Snatch didn't go anywhere without his pistol now unless it was right down the street, and he didn't like to do it then.

When he came back down the hall, Alayna was still sitting on the couch in the same outfit; he shook his head and walked outside to his old school. Snatch had a cocaine white 95 bubble caprice on 6'5. The interior was black suede with white Chanel logo all over the seats and steering wheel.

Snatch got in and waited for Alayna to come out. It was another hot and humid day. Snatch loved this kind of weather; he called it eye candy weather. Five minutes, later Alayna came strutting out.

"I thought you were going to miss your appointment because I was taking forever," Snatch asked and she rolled her eyes.

"And you not leaving me this time either. Your ass had me waiting all day to get picked up. So you're gonna have to sit in there with me." Alayna rolled her neck.

"I ain't trippin'. I wanna holla at Ming Li anyway," he grinned.

Ming Li was Alayna's homegirl who always did her nails. Snatch and Demon had fucked all of Alayna's homegirls except Ming Li. They had an ongoing bet on who would fuck her first. It was all for naught because she'd already made it clear they weren't her type and Alayna had told them that her family forbade her from dating outside of her race.

"Pssh. She definitely ain't checking for you. She got a fine-ass Chinese boyfriend," Alayna said checking her Snapchat.

They pulled up to Exclusive nails and got out.

"Hey Layna!" Ming Li squealed when they walked in.

"You get nails done too Sumayee," she joked in her heavy Chinese accent.

"Ha, ye right." Snatch eyed her.

Ming Li was winning! She was 5'0 long, silky black hair with grey streaks that fell to a heart-shaped butt that was made for a black girl's body. It wasn't big but it was just right for her slim frame.

Her succulent C cups were made to suck. And she had slanted bedroom eyes and lips that made Snatch's pole tap against his zipper every time he saw her. Ming Li was the only woman who made Snatch hesitate to holla.

"Come on." Ming Li led Alayna to her chair.

Ming Li said something to her mom in Chinese who was standing behind the cash register and they laughed, looking in Snatch's direction.

"English Ming LI!" Snatch shouted and they laughed harder.

Exclusive nails was a family ran nails shop. Everybody who worked there was Chinese. There was their mom, two sisters, Ming Li and her aunt. They'd come to America from Hong Kong ten years ago when Ming Li was nine.

They started with one nail shop and turned it into five nail shops and six beauty supply stores.

"Ming say you want paint on nails." Her mother laughed and Snatch cut his eyes at Ming Li. She and Alayna were doubled over laughing. Snatch gave them the bird and went to the bathroom. He hadn't been in the bathroom a whole minute when he heard, "Get on the floor!"

Snatch cracked the bathroom door and saw three dudes wearing shiesty masks waving guns. One of them grabbed Ming Li's mom by her hair and yelled "safe bitch, let's go" and shoved her towards the back where the bathroom was.

Snatch cocked his .45 and looked on. The dude shoved Ming Li's mom into the office. In the nail area, one was emptying the cash register and the other one was keeping an eye out the door

"You got three seconds to open this safe or I'ma put your brains all over the floor!"

"Okay, Okay! Me do what you say." She opened the floor safe and Snatch's eyes got big.

The safe had so much money in it that it was spilling over. The robber pushed her out of the way and started stuffing the money in a bag. Snatch crept out of the bathroom and into the office. The robber must've felt Snatch's presence because he turned to look over his shoulder.

BOOM! Snatch shot him before he could turn all the way around coating the money with his thoughts. Snatch came out of the office shooting the .45. Three hollow points hit the robber at the cash register square in the chest knocking him off his feet.

By the time the robber by the door started walking down on Snatch shooting a Draco, a bullet nicked Snatch's ear causing him to fall to the floor giving the would-be robber a clear shot at Snatch. But Alayna stuck her Jordan's out and tripped him sending the Draco skittering across the floor. Snatch scrambled to his feet and put in two in the robber's head.

"Come on!" Snatch yelled at Alayna.

They scrambled to the bubble and burnt rubber back to Holiday Park.

"You good?" Snatch asked Alayna when he pulled into their yard.

"No." She stuck her head out the door and threw up.

"You going to be good sis. If you hadn't tripped him, I'd probably be dead" he rubbed her back. Snatch got her in the house and to her room. He left and went and threw the gun in a pond beside colony Place.

Snatched called Demon. "Bra, some wild shit just went down."

"What?!" he asked, concerned.

Snatch relayed the events back to Demon and he said, "Go lay low at Actions and see how the jakes goin' play it."

And that's what Snatch did.

Chapter 5

"I ain't know you were a cop god" Demon joked on Snatch." It's been three days and I ain't seen or heard anything about somebody getting killed at no nail shop."

"You right." Action laughed

"Ya'll mothafuckas ain't talking about a bitch ass thing! All you gotta do is ask Alayna," Snatch said serving a fein gram.

They had finally found someone to serve them some work even though they'd gotten taxed fifteen hundred an ounce. Snatch didn't really want to do it but Action convinced him to. Action was a hood chef! She didn't hustle, she made her money on the side by cooking dope. Action had the best whip game in the state.

Snatch had seemed niggas from out town come and pay her to cook their work from them. She turned each of their ounces into an ounce and a half and it was still some pressure.

"We believe you just ain't seen nothing on the news, that's all," Demon reassured him.

"Have y'all heard about that new sports bar on Skibo Rood?" Action changed the subject.

"Yea, they say that shit be jumpin! It's owned by an old-school nigga named Dane From Bonnie Doone. He just recently came home from doing a twenty-piece," Demon said.

"What's it called?" Snatch inquired about serving another fien.

"Pandora's," Action said.

"Ohhh. That's that spot Janice wants me to take her to. They say it's a sports bar with a club feel," Snatch said.

"Here come your mom dukes." Demon pointed as Snatch's mom pulled up in her grey Chrysler 300.

"What up, Ma?" he asked walking up to the car.

"Why the hell you didn't tell me what happened at that nail salon? You got my baby scared somebody gon do something to her. And your father said he gon' call tonight at seven and he wants to speak with you."

"Tell him to hold his breath. And me telling you what happened wouldn't have solved any issues. It's ova and done with."

"Did you at least get rid of the gun?" she questioned and he nodded his head. "Okay. When you come home, we gon' have a long talk. Come give me a kiss.

Snatch kissed her on the cheek and she rode off.

"Aww," Demon teased, "the baby had to give momma a kissy, kissy." Demon and Action cracked up laughing.

"Hell, maybe if you kiss your momma more, she wouldn't be calling my phone so much," Snatch joked back, causing Action to shed tears.

"Bitch, I don't know why you are laughing. Your momma gave me half of her check every time she gets paid because I fuck her so good," Demon got on Action. They joked with each other for the next 20 minutes, each giving as good as they got. A black Mustang coming down the hill from Holland Holmes' way caught their attention.

"Who car is that?" Demon squinted, shielding his eyes from the sun with his hand.

When the mustang made it down the hill, the passenger side window rolled down and a dude came out of the window with an ARP. Cha! Cha! Cha! Rambo came out of nowhere shooting a Russian AK. Rambo chopped the mustang up killing the driver. The car came to a slow stop and the passenger tried to get up and run and Rambo filled his back up with a .223's. The trio ran over to the car and Action kicked the dude over so they could see his face.

"He's Murk Mob." Demon put his foot on the MOB tattoo on his forearm.

They walked off and looked for Rambo but didn't see him anywhere, he vanished after the shooting of the car up.

"You created a monster, my question is, are you going to be able to control him? He's like that game dog that gets that first taste of blood. Now all he wants to do is kill shit," Action said.

"He good, I got him. Besides, he's on our team, it's the otha side that needs to be worried. But anyway, I'ma bout to go by my house, I need to see what moms got goin' on." Snatch half hugged them both and stepped off.

When Snatch walked in, the blinds and curtains were closed bathing the front of the house in darkness. He reached for the light switch and his mom's voice pierced the darkness. "Leave it off and take a seat."

"Whatchu got going on, Ma? Sittin' here in the dark." His eyes adjusted to the darkness.

His mom was sitting on the couch in front of him. Snatch took a seat and waited.

"As a parent, you always want what's best for your child. You try your hardest to protect them and prepare them for this cold, harsh world. I tried to guide you away from the streets but you jumped in head first; you don't think I know what you be doing, slangin' your little rocks and shit.

Your mom has a past you know nothing about. Then you done went and got yourself in a beef that you and Demon or Action aren't prepared for. Those Murk Mob boys aren't to be played with and their babies. I was around when the Murk Mob first started," she lit a Newport 100 and inhaled.

She blew the smoke out and continued.

"Your mother was a hustler and a killa, I was *that bitch!* I had the best work in the city before your father came along. Not only was I hustling bit, I loved putting work in. With me being a woman, nigga was trying me left and right and every time they did, the city had to pull out the body bags and call the morgue.

After the fifth nigga got killed, the whole city respected my G. then your father came along; we started dating and went to the top. The friends and associates I made back then are still around and that's how I know about your illicit affairs around the city," she put him on game. "Now, about the nail salon situation......you weren't wrong because your sister was in danger, but you left one of them alive. Son, you never shoot someone without intending to kill them. A wounded person can be worse than a healthy one. Next time, ensure that the person is dead. I'm only giving you these jewels because you are set on being in the streets even though that's not the way to go. So how long do you plan on hustling?" She took some more drags from the Newport and snubbed it out in an ashtray.

"Until I get rich," he said and his mom shook her head.

"Coppin' just one ounce, it's gonna take you thirty years to do that. Furthermore, you need to ask yourself what is rich. Then ask yourself how many niggas in the game got rich and lived to tell about it. Prison or worm food is usually the end result in the street life. Your dad didn't get caught with a single piece of dope and he got a life sentence. Also, in the streets, you trust NOONE! I've seen blood brothers, niggas who came out the same pussy tell on each other to escape a prison bid. The money, clothes and hoes is all good until the judge tells you you're facing a life sentence and the mandatory minimum is twenty years in the system.

My last little bit of advice for you is to find you a real rider. A girl that ain't with you for the money and jewelry. Someone that's all the way for you and always tests the loyalty of those around you. And one last thing" his mom tossed him a wad of money. "Find you somewhere else to live. Never put your family in harm's way. You're beefing in the streets and parkin' your old school at the place you lay your head at. Son, to survive in this game, you gonna have to start using your ear or I'ma lose a son."

    His mom got up, kissed him, went to her room and closed the door, leaving Snatch to digest her words.

Chapter 6

"Dang bae! This spot is lit-lit!" Janice squeezed Snatch's hand.

They were at the sports bar Pandora's she'd been bugging him about. The place was actually straight, it wasn't what Snatch had been expecting. It was a sports bar, but it felt more than that. What Snatch really liked was that it wasn't just black people there. Every race was in attendance. Pandora's had three floors. On the first floor, there was an elevated bar that sat in the middle of the floor with flatscreens mounted about it all the way around it. And they stayed on ESPN, Fox Sports or whatever game was currently airing.

There were booths along the walls with mini TVs on the table where you could control which game you watched, and they served everything from stuffed bell peppers to salmon tacos.

Snatch and Janice walked up the steps to the second floor and a bouncer stopped them and asked for their I.D.

"You have to be eighteen to go to the next two floors and no kids," he said giving them their IDs back.

When Snatch walked onto the floor, he saw why you had to be eighteen. The first thing Snatch noticed were the uniforms the waitress wore.

All they wore were jean booty shorts and bras. They cater to the women customers too, because the men waiters wore jeans and tank tops. The next thing to hit Snatch was the weed smell. They allowed you to smoke bud in the smoker section. The second flow setup wasn't like the first floor. There was still an elevated bar, but there was a dance floor towards the back that was full of customers as they danced to Chris Brown's new single, *Nasty*. There was also a big dry eraser board that took up an entire wall where you could place bets on different games, play the pick of the week or the number board.

"This is my kinda spot," Snatch said.

"I bet it is," Janice rolled her eyes.

They grabbed a seat in a booth and grabbed the menus.

"Now, aren't you glad I convinced you to come?" Janice asked.

"Hell yea," he said sneaking a peek at the ass of a waiter.

"Are you guys ready to order?" a waitress strutted up to the table looking Snatch in the eyes ignoring Janice.

"No, but if you come back in five minutes, we will be" Janice spoke up. "Don't make me show out nigga," she threatened Snatch when the waitress walked off.

"Calm down, bae." He kissed her on the lips, mad as hell he'd brought her with him.'

Janice looked over the menu. "I want to try the shrimp enchilada."

"Order me the stuffed bell pepper and the spicy chicken wrap, I'm about to go see what's on the third floor right quick."

"Hurry back," she whined.

Snatch walked off towards the stairs. He went up the steps and got stopped by another bouncer.

"V.I.P *only*, my man. You need to talk to D-one and buy you a V.I.P. pass. Just go back to whatever floor you chillin' on, tell them you want to holla at D-one. What up Red?" the bouncer let a dude in, Snatch got a peek inside the third floor and all he heard was Future bumping out of the speakers and ass and titties. He needed to get in there, snatch went back to the second floor and told the girl behind the bar that he needed to talk to D-one.

"What's up there?" Janice inquired when he got back to the booth.

"I couldn't get in, you have to have a VIP pass," he said then saw the bartender waving him over. He got up and walked across the room.

"What up?' Snatch sat at the bar.

"You lookin' for me?" a tall light-skinned asked coming from around the bar.

"Who is you?"

"D-one."

"Ohh. Yea, I was told to talk to you about the VIP Pass." Snatch sized him up.

The dude was about 6'1 or two, with salt and pepper dreads that hung below his waist. He had to weigh a good two-sixty.

"Okay. A week pass is two grand, and a month pass is five grand, I don't do them for any less than a week or for longer than a month."

"What's so good about the third floor?" Snatch was curious because that was a nice piece of change to be spending not knowing what you were gonna get

"Everything you can think of depending on the day. There could be a high roller poker game or spades or tank games. Costume parties, man, it ain't no telling. And shots are on the house but if you want a bottle, you'll have to pay." D-one gave him the spill.

Snatch was about to ask him another question when someone walked through the door and caught a glimpse of Chance walking up the stairwell.

"I'll get back with you on that." Snatch ran off.

Snatch got to the stairs just as Chance and a group of Murk Mob niggas disappeared on the third floor.

Snatch walked back to his and Janice's booth. "Janice, we gon' have to do this another time."

"No the fuck, we not! What you're about to do is sit your yellow ass down and we're goin' to enjoy our food," she told him not knowing that they were in danger.

Snatch chuckled and said "okay."

He texted Demon and told him where he was at and that Chance was there. Demons' response was that he was on the way. Snatch cocked his Glock and sat it on his lap.

"Guess what boo?" Janice said excitedly.

"What?" Snatch asked.

"I got accepted to Harvard! Your girl is gonna be a lawyer." She beamed.

"That's what's up. I'm proud of you, girl. When does the semester start?" He ate some of his tenders.

"Next month. You coming with me right?" Her eyes searched his.

"Janice….you know I can't leave the city yet. I got a lot goin' on and I can't dip out on Demon and Action right now. Besides, I would be a distraction more than anything."

"What is there for you in Fayetteville except trouble? A new scene might do you some good. A place where nobody knows you, it'll just be me and you." She grabbed his hand.

Her pitch sounded good to Snatch's ears but he was a Fayetteville nigga through and through. He'd only been outside of the city a few times and that had been to see his da. He didn't count the times that he'd been to Raeford, Spring Lake or the little cities that surrounded Fayetteville because those cities were only five-minute drives. Snatch didn't really even like leaving his side of town.

"And who'd watch out for Alayna?" he questioned and she got quiet.

"Exactly. Go ahead bae, it ain't like you leaving the state."

"Huh? Baby, Harvard is in Massachusetts, we not gonna be able to see each other like that anymore. I know how these thirsty ass hoes are and I'm not trying to lose my spot." She searched his face for some reassurance but he didn't give her any.

Snatch wasn't going to give her any false hope, he didn't know what the future held. He didn't even know if he was going to be alive to see his next birthday.

"No one knows the future, Janice. Now as far as losing your spot. Janice, other than my momma and Alayna, you're the only other woman I love. Now, don't let that go to your head. But your spot is cemented here." he took her hand and placed it over his heart. The future is …bae I'ma be honest; I can't promise I'll be alive tomorrow. I live for the day fuck tomorrow." Snatch gave it to her straight with no chaser.

"Oh my God, don't talk like that. You have so much potential Sumajee. You're not like the rest of them boys in the hood; you graduated at the top of your class. You're smart enough to do anything you want. And I love you too" she said with tears in her eyes.

Demon sent Snatch a text saying he was outside. "Come on, we'll talk about this later." They paid the bill and left.

Demon flashed his lights when they walked out.

"Here go my keys, I'll call you later."

"No, what are you about to do?"

"Janice, what I tell you about that? Just do what I told you."

She kissed him and went and got in his bubble. Snatch went and got in the passenger seat of the Durango Demon was in. Snatch smiled when he looked in the backseat and saw Action and Rambo. Rambo had twin desert eagles on his lap. Rambo's black eyes were gleaming. Rambo's brown skin looked like it was glowing; at 5'7, he was tall for a twelve-year-old. Rambo had curly black hair that he usually kept in braids but tonight, it was all over his head. Rambo had sharp features. His nose was sharp and slim, he had close-set eyes, high cheeks and medium-sized lips. Snatch kept looking him in the eyes trying to put his finger on the look Rambo had on his face.

"You love this shit, don't you?" Snatch asked him.

"I like spinning and stepping more than I like getting my dick wet."

Snatch smiled because he knew now that Rambo was a killa's killa.

"So what happened in there?" Action inquired rubbing her pink .45 with the switch on it.

Snatch told them what happened.

"So we gotta wait for them to come out?" Rambo was anxious to murk something.

"Pretty much," Snatch said

Action rolled up a backwood filled with oud and passed it around.

"That's the nigga D-one that own the spot," Demon said pointing.

D-one left out the front door and walked in their direction.

"What's up with dude?" Rambo cocked the De's

"Chill," Demon stated.

D-one walked up to the Durango and tapped on the glass

"What it do, Og?" Demon asked rolling his window down.

D-one looked in the Durango, looked at everybody and his eyes stopped on Snatch.

"Now, I'm a street nigga myself and four motherfuckas sittin' in a car with pistols on their laps can only mean one thing. Somebody is about to lose their life. I respect the game and I'm not going to tell you what to do but what I do ask is that you don't do it in my parking lot. A body here will affect my business. Real nigga to real nigga," he said, never taking his eyes off of Snatch,

"We got you O.G." Demon crunk the jeep up and parked at the McDonalds across the street.

"I can't believe y'all let him make y'all move," Rambo said.

"He didn't make us do anything. He asked us and here's a lesson to you: Every battle isn't worth fighting. Getting into it with him wouldn't have benefitted us at all. Focus.

You have to focus on the task at hand," Snatch gave Rambo a jewel.

They smoked three more backwoods waiting for Chance to come out. It wasn't until three-thirty that people came filing out. By this time, the roads were clear, the only people out were third shifters, club goers and people going to after-hours spots.

"He got in that tan Challenger." Demon started pulling out.

Chance pulled out with two other Challengers falling in behind him. Demon pulled up beside Chance's car. Snatch and Rambo rolled their windows down and commenced to sending Chance to the afterlife. BOOM! BOOM! BOOM! The desert eagles were sounding off. After the first few shots, Chance's Challenger swerved off the road and smacked a light pole. Then they focused their attention on the remaining challengers. They were only able to do damage to one of them before they saw blue lights approaching.

"Get us back to the hood!" Snatch yelled.

"Ain't gotta worry about that pussy no more," Rambo said.

"Facts. Drop me off at Janice's," Snatch said.

Later that night, Snatch fucked Janice and slept like a baby knowing he had taken Chance out of the game.

Chapter 7

Snatch woke up the next morning without a worry in the world. He took a shower and got ready for the day. Ever since having the talk with his mother, he'd moved out and was staying with Janice until he found his own spot. Snatch looked at his G-shock and saw that it was only 8:30 in the morning. Janice was still lying in bed asleep. He threw on a pair of black gym shorts, a white wife beater and some black air max 95's. Snatch was about to go gab Demon and hit the block up, he needed to get off his last fourteen grams.

"Where you going?" Janice's little brother Jason asked when Snatch came out of Janice's room.

"To mind my business, you need to get you some?" Snatch ruffled his hair.

Jason was thirteen and looked like he could've been Janice's son because they favored each other so much. They had the same dark brown skin, light brown eyes and dow-shaped eyes.

"I got some business." He grinned at Snatch. "Me and Alayna have some special business we need to attend to." He took off running. Snatch took off after him but Jason got out the front door and ran down the street.

"You can run but you can't hide!" Snatch yelled after him and he gave Snatch a finger.

Snatch went back in the house, popped some pink molly and grabbed his pistol. He still wasn't going anywhere without his fire. Snatch hopped the fence in his mom's backyard and came out on Demon's Street. Snatch walked around to the back and let himself into Demon's room.

They had converted their garage into a bedroom, Demon's bedroom. Demon wasn't in his room, so Snatch walked into the house and still didn't see him.

"Sumajee, what are you doing here?" Demon's mom walked out of her bedroom.

"My bad, Ms. Evette, I'm looking for Demon."

"He left out about an hour ago," she told him

"Okay." He turned to leave

"You got some weed, boy?"

"Yea, why?"

"Because yo ass is about to smoke a blunt with me then you can go find that boy of mine." She turned to go back into her room.

It was then that Snatch noticed the flimsy robe that she had on only covered half of her ass. He averted his eyes but not before he got a peek at Everett's ample backside, Ms. Evette was strapped in every department. She had D cups breasts and hips, thigs and ass for days! Evette had a smooth midnight-black skin tone and sensual features. She wasn't all that in the face but she was far from ugly. She was a young thirty-two, she'd had Demon when she was only fourteen.

"Here boy!'

Snatch walked into her room and she had a vanilla dutch in her outstretched hand. She had also put on some black biker shorts. Snatch leaned against the dresser and rolled up while she flipped through the channels on the TV.

"So you and my son gon sell drugs y'all whole life?" she asked watching Snatch light the blunt.

The molly had kicked in and Snatch was feeling himself to the tenth power. He shrugged his shoulders and passed her the blunt. She took a pull and started coughing. "Weak ass lungs." Snatch laughed feeling the effects of the potent weed.

"Boy, I was smokin' before you were alive. And since you talking that hot shit, come over and let me blow you a shotgun."

Snatch walked over to the bed and let her blow him a shotgun.

"And hold it lil nigga" she took two hits.

Snatch held the smoke in until he couldn't then blew it in the air.

"Like I said, weak ass lungs," he said then the weed hit like a heavyweight boxer. Snatch had to lean up against the dresser. He was astronaut high! The weed and molly had him high, high such that the room was spinning! Snatch wiped his hand down his face and Evette started laughing.

"Yo ass blitzed." She smiled, high as hell herself. Snatch already felt like he was God's gift to women and the molly was intensifying it. His eyes traveled from her face down to the gap between her legs. The gap between her legs was so wide you could stick your hand through and not touch her thighs. "Boy! Yeah, it's time for you to go, you trippin!" Evette screwed her face up seeing his pole pressing up against his shorts.

The molly had Snatch on some freaky shit, he pulled his wife beater off and tugged his shorts down.

"Have you lost your mind! Sumayee!" she stood up.

Snatch closed the distance between them and kissed her aggressively.

"It's just me and you, ain't nobody gon know you let this young, fine nigga fuck ya brains out" he whispered in her ear and grabbed c handful of her ass.

"This never leaves this room," she said lust consuming her as she eyed his chiseled body. Evette dropped down into a squat and pulled his briefs down, freeing Snatch's rock hard pole. "You hard as hell." She licked around the head.

Snatch pushed her robe off her shoulders and caressed her breast. He was at a loss for words. He couldn't believe Evette's tick ass was about to give him some pussy. She grabbed his dick at the base and slid it into her mouth three quick times.

"Stop playin'." Snatch grabbed her by the back of her lace front.

He guided her mouth to his dick. He took a hold of her lace front with both hands and started fucking her mouth. Everett relaxed her throat muscles and took Snatch's pole down her throat every time he stroked without a problem.

"Watch out." She pushed him backwards. "Get on the bed."

Snatch got on the bed and lay back. He stroked his dick up and down while she pulled off her biker shorts. Evette straddled him and guided his dick into her with her hand.

"Damn boy," she gasped sinking down until he was all the way in.

Demon's mom's cat was pressure! Her muscles gripped Snatch like she had a hand down there. "Ride this dick!" Snatch slapped her on the ass as she swiveled her hips.

He palmed both of her ass cheeks while she rode him.

"Pinch my nipples!" she gasped, grabbing two handfuls of her hair. He reached up and took both of her nipples in his hands and rolled them between his fingers. "Yess boy!" she moaned.

Snatch took one of his hands and started rubbing her clit up and down.

"Uhnn!" Her eyes rolled into the back of her head as her orgasm rocked her body. She collapsed on Snatch's chest. He spread her cheeks apart and started pushing his hips up off the mattress, putting his entice ripe up into her.

"Sumajee, Sumajee" she whispered in his ear and bit down on his neck.

Snatch picked his pace up, going into overdrive.

"Arrrgh," he growled releasing into Evette

"Mmm!" She looked down into Snatch's face and kissed him. "You got my pussy thumpin'! Oh my god, you're still hard." She lifted up off of him, seeing Snatch's pole standing at attention. "I can't let you leave like that. Come beat this pussy up." She stood in the middle of the floor, grabbed her ankles and started making her ass wobble.

Her ass was moving every which way. Snatch got up and got behind her. He slid in and felt like he'd gone to heaven. Snatch fucked her nonstop for the next hour and a half, putting her to sleep with her thumb in her mouth. He looked down at his phone as a text came through from Alayna.

//: *911! Come home quick!*

Chapter 8

Snatch broke his neck rushing out of Demon's house! Alayna never sent him texts in that manner. Snatch hopped the fence and came in through his mom's backdoor with his pistol up and ready.

"Alayna!" he yelled

"In the living room!"

Snatch rushed into the living room and saw Alayna sitting down with Ming Li laughing and joking.

"What was 911?"

"Ming Li needs to talk to you." Alayna looked at Ming Li

"Hi Sumajee!" she waved

"What up Ming Li?" Snatch was curious as to why she needed to talk to him.

He hadn't seen her since the nail shop incident.

"You need to come with me." She got up and walked towards the front door.

"Where to?" Snatch didn't move

"Just come, me mom want to talk to yo." Snatch followed Ming Li out of the house and to her Lexis LC 500 coupe.

"What do your mom want?"

"You see," she grinned.

Snatch sat back, let her drive and listened to Nicki Minaj talk shit on her new track.

"Whatchu know about Nicki Minaj?" Snatch questioned.

"Nicki me bitch! Her alter ego Chun Li is me." She waved her finger in the air for emphasis.

They bull-shitted around until they pulled into China Wok and parked.

"Come on." Ming Li got out.

Snatch followed her into the Chinese restaurant. Ming Li said something to the girl behind the counter in Chinese and kept walking. Ming led Snatch to the second floor and to the back where her mother was sitting at ta table drinking sake. She got up and wrapped Snatch in a hug.

"Thank you. Leave us." Ming Li bowed and walked off. "That was a noble deed you did. Not many would have done that. You have a warrior spirit. You save family and I have to repay you."

"No, you're good—" he said and she put her hand up stopping him.

"It is right thing to do." She looked at something behind Snatch causing him to turn around.

Snatch looked and saw a Chinese man of average height in black slacks, black dress shirt and some black loafers walking in their direction.

"Sumajee, this is my son, Yuki. Yuki, this is Sumajee. Now, I leave you two." She walked off.

Snatch had never seen Yuki before. Yuki was about 5'9 fit with long black hair pulled back into a ponytail and a nose ring. To Snatch, he looked like an average Chinese dude. He sat down across from Snatch and stared at him.

Snatch sat there matching his stare for a few seconds before saying "Bra what up? I ain't into having a staring contest."

"I'm trying to figure out why you chose to risk your life for my family. You don't seem like the type." Yuri turned his head as if examining Snatch. Yuki had a voice that was robotic sounding.

"My baby sister was there too."

"But she was safe. They were focused on the door, the cash register, and the safe. I watched the security cameras."

"I don't know how shit goes in China, but I've seen robberies turn to rape and murder charges more times than I can count. So, I wasn't about to wait for things to get out of hand. Need I remind you that he had your mother in the office by himself?" Snatch was starting to feel like he was being interrogated. "I'm outta here." He stood up.

"You can learn a lot about a person by the way they handle certain situations. Your impatience isn't a good trait to have, nor is your misplaced compassion." He stood up fluidly. "Aggression is good to a certain degree but if you use your mind in the correct fashion, you'll never have to use your aggression. Also, aggression is a precursor to violence, something of a warning. Let the violence come first and you'll almost always win because it wasn't expected. Surprise attacks are the key. Come, let me show you something."

Yuki led Snatch through the kitchen to the back into a big room that they used for killing and chopping up meat.

"What the fuck?!" Snatch said.

There was a naked black dude suspended in the air by his arms.

"This is who survived," Yuki told him.

Snatch moved closer and saw that the man's skin had been stripped off from the waist down.

"And your reason for showing me this is" Snatch wasn't really impressed.

Yuki looked at Snatch with a smirk on his face.

"You have exterior of stand-up guy, but is your heart cut the same? Before he died, he told me everything I wanted to know and a little more. China has the best torture methods known to man."

"I ain't come here to see or hear none of this bullshit! You ain't the only one cut from that gangsta cloth." Snatch walked out.

"Sumajee!" Ming Li smiled when she saw him, but his cold look wiped the smile off of her face. Snatch walked out of the restaurant and started texting Demon to see where he was at. He looked back and saw Ming Li's mom walking up McPherson Church Road trying to get as far away from Yuki as possible. He wanted to push Yuki's hairline back. The more he thought about it, the madder he got.

"Fuck that!" Snatch turned around and headed back in the direction of the China Wok. Snatch was about to show Yuki how American gangstas gave it up. A grey Nissan GT-R pulled in front of him, cutting him off. The window rolled down as Snatch was upping his pistol. "Just the motherfucka I was looking for." Snatch sneered bringing the Glock up.

"Sumajeeno! Ming Li's face appeared beside Yuki's making Snatch slow up. "Get in please! It's important," she said.

Snatch reluctantly climbed into the backseat behind Yuki, his pistol on his lap.

"I don't know what happened between you two but it's over. Excuse him because he's naturally suspicious and overprotective of us. Now my family wanted you to come by the restaurant to show you your appreciation for what you did. Look in that bookbag, you can either take the money or the drugs. Your sister told me that you be hustling, so that was put in there in case you would rather have it instead" Ming Li had turned in her seat to face Snatch.

Snatch looked in the bookbag and saw what looked to be about thirty racks and a block of raw. He grabbed the work and put it in his pocket. Ming Li nodded her head.

"Sumajee, I'm 14K, the third largest triad in the world. I have an unlimited supply of drugs. Do right and you'll be rich beyond your wildest dreams." Yuki said. Nothing else was said as they drove him back to his hood.

They dropped him off in Colony Place. He went and knocked on Action's door. Her mom opened the door in her house coat.

"She's in her room." She let him in.

Action's mom, Alice was cool as a fan. She let them do whatever they wanted. She was a recovering drug addict, she'd been sobered for six months and was starting to get her weight back. Alice had dropped down to a skinny ninety pounds now; she was about one-fifty. Action and her mom were twins. When she gained her weight back, it was going to be hard to tell them apart. The real difference was that Action had a little more ass. Snatch walked down the hall to Action's room and walked in.

"Damn mothafucka! Do you know how to knock?" She covered her breast with her hands.

"Fuck all that, what can you do with this?" he gave her the work.

"How much is this?" she asked turning the work over in her hand. Her exposed breast forgotten about.

"I'm about to put it on the scale now"

They put the block on the scale and it read five hundred and four grams. Action opened the package and immediately knew that it wasn't cocaine as they had thought.

"That's heroin, Snatch"

They had never dealt with heroin, all they messed with was coke.

"I'm about to take this back," Snatch said.

"No, you not, do you know how much money you can make off this in a short period of time especially if it's some fire?" Action said.

"We need to see how good it is then."

"Old man Willie do it?" she said.

"What's the biz?" Demon walked into the room.

"Check this shit out, bitch" Snatch waved him over. "That's a half a birdie boy!" Snatch dapped him up slapping Demon's hand quick and hard.

"This gon' put us all the way in the game. Ain't no lookin' back now." Demon visualized the money they were about to make.

"It's heroin though, we about to get Willie to try it and see how good it is." Action pulled a yellow American Eagle shirt over her head.

Snatch cracked about a gram off of the block and put the rest of it up. They walked to Willie's apartment and knocked on the door.

"What is it?" Willie's daughter answered the door.

"Is your dad here?" Snatch questioned.

"No, why? What y'all want with him?" she put her hand on her hip.

"I needed him to try something for me but you can do it instead," Action said walking into the apartment.

Snatch and Demon walked in behind her and formed a half circle around Willie's daughter as she sat on the couch.

"Let me see it," she said

Snatch put about a point four on the table. She used her ID and crushed the white powder down into a line. She rolled a twenty dollar bill up and snorted the line. It wasn't a whole minute before her nose started bleeding and she started acting like she was having a seizure. Demon and Snatch just looked at her because they didn't know what to do. Action ran and got a pitcher of ice water and threw it in her face. She gasped, stopped spasming, started taking big deep breaths then passed out.

"Is she breathing?" Demon questioned

"I don't know." Snatch left out of the apartment. They went back to Action's leaving behind no evidence that they had been in Willie's apartment.

"It's too strong," Action said.

"We need to cut it, but not too much; that way, the *fiens* will keep coming," Demon added.

They spent the next few hours on the internet trying to find out about heroin and how to cut it when it came to Snatch.

"I'll be back."

Snatch went home to ask his momma. She was sitting in the dining room smoking a Newport and sipping a glass of wine.

"Ma, what all do you know about heroin?"

"A lot, why?" she asked and he told her he had come across some and didn't know how to cut it. "Let me see it."

She stuck her pinky nail in the dope and touched her tongue.

"Son, this is China white and it's the closest thing to pure boy I've seen in years. You can put a two on an ounce and still have the fiens goin' crazy."

"What you mean a two?"

"You can put two ounces of cut on an ounce and turn one ounce into three."

"But what do we cut it with?" he asked thinking that they could turn the eighteen onions into fifty-four.

"The best thing to use is Miralax or Benita, either one will do."

Snatch went back and told them all the information that he'd gotten. They went to the grocery store and bought both.

"Let me do this." Action put a surgical mask over her face and turned into a chemist. She was going to cut one ounce with the Miralax and one with the Benita. Whichever one the fiens liked the most was the one they were going to stick with. Demon and Snatch smoked a blunt watching Action do her thing.

"How'd you run across this?" Demon asked.

"The nail shop" Snatch laughed.

"Nail shop, nigga go head."

"Nah, for real," Snatch said then gave him the rundown on how he got it.

"He the plug, plug bitch! Count up!" Demon clapped his hands.

"We about to turn this bitch out, we really the who's who's now." Snatch smiled.

"Okay, check 'em out." Action held up two powder-filled Ziploc bags.

"Let's go," Snatch said.

Snatch drove to Bonnie Doone, one of the hoods in Fayetteville that he knew heroin users to be. He turned off the Blvd. onto Johnson Street and cruised down the road. He turned onto Higgins Street and saw a group of junkies.

"Aye come ere!" Demon yelled to the group.

"Try this for me and tell me what you think." Snatch gave all of them a bag making sure he paid attention to which one's he gave certain bags to. The six fiens pulled syringes out of their pockets and put their kits together. The trio watched the junkies shoot up and instantly go into nods. Of the six, two of them got to shaking and foaming at the mouth. The remaining four said that it was the best boy they'd ever had. They gave them more dope and told them when they came back to have their money right.

"Action uses the Benita," Snatch told her because the Benita bags were the bags that the two fiens od'd on.

They stopped at an Arab store and got a box of wax baggies to bag up with. They were officially on the road to riches.

Chapter 9

Snatch and Demon hit the ground running! The dope was so good the fiens were blowing their phones up nonstop. They were turning Colony Place into a million-dollar trap. In two weeks, they had sold all fifty-four ounces and had orders for a half of a brick worth of sales. Twenty fiens had overdosed in the projects and when word got out about the heroin causing fiens to o'd, they started coming from all over the city to get their fix.

"I don't see why we can't be millionaires in about a year," Demon said, counting his money a year. "A year? My nigga, in a year, we're gonna be multimillionaires! Snatched corrected, formulating a master plan in his mind.

Snatch had visions of them at the top of the game, taking trips overseas, fucking foreign bitches and sailing on the Atlantic Ocean on mega yachts.

"I'm meeting Yuki, later on, to discuss what he gonna be charging us per brick," Snatch told Demon. "I hit you before I leave." He walked out of the feins spot.

Snatch had to go by Janice's house. She was leaving for Harvard today and he had to see her off. He made the short drive to her house, where she was outside with her mother.

"Hey Ms. Jackie," Snatch said

"What are we gonna do without my baby?" Janice's mom's eyes watered,

"We gon' survive," Snatch reassured her, wrapping an arm around her.

"I bet." Janice twisted her lips up.

Snatch walked over to Janice and wrapped her up in a bear hug. She melted in his arms.

"Baby, please come with me," Janice pleaded looking up into his face.

"We already went through this. I'm gon be coming up there plus you need me here more. I gotta watch after yo mom and Jason." Snatch slid five bands into her clutch.

"How often am I goin' to be able to see you?" she inquired.

"At least twice a month," Snatch said kissing her on the forehead.

Janice accepted his answer and helped him put the last of her bags in the car.

"Promise me that I'm still gonna be your girl when I get back."

"Janice, you'll always be my girl." Snatch gave her some closure

Snatch really, really fucked with Janice; he loved her but things were finally looking up for him and he couldn't allow this once-in-a-lifetime opportunity to slip by. "I'll be back to visit for Christmas too." Janice slid her tongue into Snatch's mouth.

They shared one last passionate kiss, then Janice hugged her mom and Jason then got in her car and drove off to start a new chapter in her life. Snatch watched her drive away. He was secretly hurt, he was just too much of a gangsta to allow a tear to escape his eye.

"If y'all need anything, just call," Snatch told Ms. Jackie before getting into his old school.

As Snatch got to the exit of Holiday Park, Yuki called him.

"Come to the restaurant so we can talk," Yuki told Snatch and hung up

Snatch shook his head and texted Demon, telling him to meet him at the China Wok. Snatch felt like a kid on

Christmas Eve. It was every dope boy's dream to meet a real connect. Not only has Snatch met a connect but the connect was in a way indebted to him because of his good deed. If the meeting with Yuki turned out the way Snatch wanted it, Demon and Action were going to be dope boy royalty. When Snatch pulled into the parking lot, Demon was posted up on his black Demon. Snatch parked beside him and got out.

"You ready, my nigga?" Snatch questioned.

"When am I ever not ready?" Demon smirked.

"Let's get to it then."

"Hey Sumajee!" Ming Li squealed when they walked into the restaurant. "Hi Mr….." she looked at Demon.

"Demon," he said staring at her.

"Right this way." She led them upstairs to a back table.

Ming Li was looking fine as ever wearing a red and gold Kimona. Even under the loose robe, her little butt poked out.

"I thought you were Chinese, why are you wearing a Kimono?" Snatch asked Ming Li knowing that Kimonas were a Japenases garmet.

"Me am but that not mean me don't like wearing nice things. Me don't care who it come from. Look good right?" She turned on her heels.

Snatch chuckled and nodded his head.

"I go get Yuki"

Both Snatch and Demon stared as she strutted away.

"Wifey material," Snatch said.

"Times ten," Demon agreed taking a seat.

They had to wait a full fifteen minutes before Yuki appeared.

"Who is this?" Yuki looked Demon up and down.

"This is Demon, my right-hand man," said Snatch.

"Never let your right hand know what your left hand is doing. So if you'll excuse us Demon we have some business to attend to" Yuki dismissed Demon.

"Obviously, you have your people fucked up. But I forgive you because you don't know any better. Respect isn't given away, it has to be earned. So keep that in mind the next time you address me," Demon said coldly but Snatch knew he was big mad.

"No, you keep that in mind the next time you address someone that's above your tax bracket boy," Yuki set Demon off.

"Wait! Wait!" Snatch yelled knowing Demon was about to put their meal tickets brain all over the restaurant tables.

"You better get your people before they make the front page. I don't even know why he's here," Yuki said evenly.

"Because I brought him, that's why! So, you need to give him the same respect that you give me," Snatch stated.

"I'm doing business with you and you only. What you do and who you deal with is on you but I won't be taking part in it. So, what are you going to do, get rich beyond your wildest dreams or stay broke because I don't want to deal with your homie?" Yuki quizzed.

Snatch looked at Demon. Snatch was willing to walk out the door with his dog. He wanted to get rich but not at the expense of his day one. Snatch's loyalty ran deeper than that.

"Handle that B.I. I'll be outside." Demon brushed past Yuki and walked out.

Snatch sat back down followed by Yuki.

"You made a wise decision Snatch," said Yuki.

"I didn't make shit! Demon did because if he would been on Demon time, your thoughts would been all over the carpet. It's loyalty over everything with me, keep that in mind when dealing with me" Snatch put it out there.

Yuki steepled his hands and sat them in front of his face with his chin resting on his thumbs.

"It's not what you see that you should fear but what you don't. A person only shows you what they want you to see. Case in point. You see me by myself all the time, but a man of my caliber has to have a team, or he'd be an easy target right?" Yuki relaxed in his chair and said something in Chinese.

Out of nowhere, several hard-looking Chinese dudes appeared from every direction each one carrying some sort of weapon.

"So, you see, you might've killed me, but they would've hurt you just enough to subdue you then they would've made you watch while they tortured your family. Snatch, I'm going to charge you twenty-five a brick but the least you can get after this first round is twenty and after five re-ups, you'll have to cop a minimum of fifty. Can you handle that?" Yuki inquired and Snatch nodded his head "You need to assemble you a solid team and remember that a chain is only so strong as its weakest link. You have a gift on your passenger seat," he said and casually walked away.

Snatch went outside to his old school and saw two China Wok bags on the passenger seat.

"Did you see who put these here?" Snatch asked Demon and he shook his head. "We are getting a bird for twenty-five but we have to cop at least a sub" Snatch gave Demon the particulars.

"Snatch, after we get rich, rich I'ma kill that slant-eyed muthafucka," Demon said.

"And I'll be the one to set him up."

Chapter 10

Yuki had blessed him with five bricks of China white on consignment, so all they owed him was a hundred and twenty-five thousand. They'd made a hundred and fifty thousand off the work that they'd already moved, so they could easily pay him off now. But Snatch wanted to flip the work that they'd just got, then pay what they wanted. That way, they wouldn't owe shit. Snatch dropped the five bricks off to Action and told her to do her thing. He knew when she got done, they were going to have fifteen bricks of fire! Snatch did the math and knew they were going to clear one paint five million off the fifteen. Snatch and Demon now had the best work in the city and the best prices. While everyone else was selling twenty dollars a point, they were selling ten dollars a point, cut-throating the competition.

"Bra, we hold all the cards, niggas is gon' have to march to our beat. Everybody about to be trying to jump on our dick now that we got the wave but that's dead. If you ain't been here, then fuck ya two times!?" Demon rasped.

"Whateva you say goes bro. Look tho, we need to put a squad together. We can't be everywhere at once and I'm not trying to miss a red penny, and the way I'm envisioning shit, it's gonna be monumented. Like we about to be kingpin status! We about to turn Colony Place into the Carter from New Jack City. But that's just gonna be our headquarters. I want to supply all the major hoods from Massey Hill, Bonnie

Doone, Deept Creek Road, 301, Ramsey Street and the Murk," Snatch said.

"Them Murk Mob nigga is gonna be a problem but not a problem we can't handle. Our bad about to be out this world. So we gon be able to control the hood economy and whoever controls the economy controls the hood," Demon stated.

"How tho?" questioned Snatch. #

"Y'all got some loud?" Ms. Evette poked her head into Demon's room.

"Here." Snatch pulled out eight white runts. Thank you, baby. She crabbed the gas, ran her nails along Snatch's palm and winked.

She made her ass wobble as she left out. Snatch looked at Demon to see if he saw him staring at his mom's ass. But he wasn't paying any attention. Ever since Snatch had fucked Evette, they had been sneaking around fucking every chance they got.

"How we're going to secure the economy is by doing what you just said and make everyone cop from us. We're getting top-grade dope for next to nothing. We can sell weight to all the heavy hitters in each hood at a price that they can't refuse. We're not gonna be able to set up our people in every hood. Some niggas ain't going, he is having that." Demon gave his insight,

"They not gon have no choice! Get down or get laid down."

"I agree some hoods are worth taking over but a lot are not. Why not let the niggas that the fiens Snatch mulled it over for a quick second and realized that Demon had a valid point."

"But what hoods are we gonna take control of?" Snatch inquired.

"Moosey Hill, Shaw Road, Savory Heights, Hollywood Heights, all of downtown, Tapeka Heights, Meadowwood the hill and Ramsey Street," Demon said causing Snatch to whistle.

"Then some hoods that are gonna take a war or two to take over," Snatch said.

"Not necessarily, but if, so be it. Now how are we gonna build this team?" And what are we gonna call it?"

"Of course me, you and Action are at the top of the food chain. Rambo gon' be out shooter, he go handle security and the lookouts. Then we gon' have out under bosses which I think should be the ones who handle the day-to-day shit and report back to us. Under them will be the workers and runners; they'll report to the underbosses. Everyone's loyalty will be tested on the regular. The very first sign of disloyalty or weaknesses to be shown will be rewarded with death. I watched my pops go to prison because his man got caught with some work and folded. I can't and won't make that same mistake," said Snatch.

I feel you, once a few examples get made, people will either fall in line or be a memory. What's the first hood you want to go to?" Asked Demon.

"We got our shit runnin' correct first, then we got to brunch out. Count up boys is the name" Snatch looked down at his phone as a text came through from Demon's mom.

Evette: You need to ditch him, the back of my throat needs some attention.

Snatch: Where you at??

Evette: In my room playin' with ur pussy"

Snatch: Let me see

Evette: Sent Snatch a picture of her in the bed with two fingers inside her love box.

"I'm bout to get in the shower, whatchu about to do?" Demon asked

"Bet" Demon grabbed his shower shit and walked to the shower.

Snatch waited until he heard the shower cut on and crept to Evette's room and clashed the door.

"What took you so long?" she sat up in the bed. Snatch stepped out of his shorts already hard and grabbed the back of her head. She didn't have to be told what to do, she went into freak mode.

"That's right......suck daddy's dick." Snatch watched as Evette went in, bobbing her head on his pole in circles.

She pulled Snatch out of her mouth and slapped her tongue with his wood. She licked around the head and kissed it.

"Fuck me boy" she laid back on the bed motioning Snatch to her with her finger.

Snatch knows he was wrong because Demon was right down the hall in the shower. But Evette's pussy was so good he couldn't resist. He crawled into the bed and entered her forbidden place.

'This pussy so fuckin' wet and tight," he growled in her ear while stroking her.

"And it's all yours," Evette moaned, lifting her hips up so that Snatch could go deeper.

Snatch grabbed her left leg and lifted it up so he could pound her at a better angle. Snatch sped his strokes up, he was trying to get his nut off and be gone before Demon got out of the shower,

"I'm cum all over this dick!" Evette moaned digging her nails into Snatch's back.

"Shh!" Snatch put his hand over her mouth.

"Mmm! Mmm! Mmm!" Evette moaned through his hand.

Her body looked up and her eyes rolled into the top of her head. Snatch felt her gushing all over his dick. He shortened his strokes up but started going faster rushing his nut.

"Damn!" he collapsed on top of her

"Your young ass gon drive me crazy." She licked his ear.

Snatch didn't want to move, he wanted to go to sleep but he heard the shower cutting off. He jumped up, put on his clothes, looked down at Evette's naked frame one last time and left. Snatch needed to leave Evette alone, but her sex game wouldn't allow it. He just had to keep being slick so Demon never got wind of him fucking his mother.

Chapter 11

Action turned the five bricks into fifteen, now all they had to do was put it out. Snatch wanted to get their team organized before they opened up shop.

"What exactly is my position going to be?" Action questioned smoking a blunt of loud. "Being a boss, cutting the work and whatever else you want to do. You're an integral part of this operation. Everyone has a part to play. Me, you and Demon are the heart of the organization. Whatever we say goes. And where the fuck is Demon? He should have been here a minute ago." Snatch looked out the blinds in Action's window.

"He gon' be here, you know he not gon miss this meeting. But while we wait, let me get some of that dick" Action grabbed Snatch's dick through his jeans.

Nobody knew that Snatch fucked Action on the regular and so did Demon. But it wasn't only when Snatch or Demon wanted to fuck, if Action got horny, she would make one of them come give her some dick. Snatch was Action's first piece of dick, he'd popped her cherry back in the day, then put Demon on. They were the only two dudes that she let fuck her. Action ran through dudes the way Snatch ran through bitches. She'd have a boyfriend for a month or two then ditch them the minute they pressed her too hard for some pussy.

The closest her boyfriends got to fucking her was eating her pussy. They were definitely dead on getting their dick sucked. The closest Snatch had gotten Action to sucking his dick was a night when they were smoking and popping molly. And all she'd done that night was lick around the head of it, then Action was the type of white girl that only dated black dudes.

"Hurry up!" she demanded.

Snatch grabbed Action, spun her around roughly and bent her over the bed. He yanked the legging down over her juicy thighs and ass and slapped her on the butt leaving a red handprint.

"I'ma fuck you up" Action looked back over her shoulder at Snatch.

"Not before I fuck you up" he grinned pulling his pole out. Action had a pretty, fat cat! If he'd had more time, Snatch woulda eat her. He rubbed the head of his dick up and down her center teasing her.

"Put it in" she whined reaching back, grabbing Snatch's wood and backing up on it.

"Thirsty ass" he laughed pushing all the way in until his pelvis was up against her ass.

He pulled all the way out and slammed back into her causing her to raise up on her toes, trying to run.

"Not today" Snatch grabbed two handfuls of her long blonde hair and began to drive his hips forward.

"Snatch! Snatch!" Action moaned.

"Fuck!" Snatch pulled out seeing Demon's new Cadillac pull into the parking lot.

"I know your lame ass ain't nut that fast" Action twisted her face up.

"Yea right. Demon just pulled up. We got to have this meeting. After we get done I'ma finish yo ass off real proper" he fixed his jeans and walked out the room.

He met Demon before he could get to the steps

"What took you so long?"

"I got caught up in the middle of some drama," he said.

"Well, we got a meeting with Trey, Tasha, Zay and Lil Buck at the park in five minutes, come on." They walked the short walk to the park and met Zay, Tasha, Trey and Buck. The foursome were hustlers' hustlers. Their hustle was strong. They'd been hustling ever since Snatch could remember. With their hustle game, Snatch knew with the right work, they'd take off to the moon. He also knew that they were the type of people that if you put them on, they would forever be loyal. Zay was a tall Gucci mane lookalike that Snatch went to school with.

He even could rap a little bit. But his grind game was legendary! He'd gone from a gram to a quarter bird in two weeks and he hadn't looked back since. Trey was a twenty-two-year-old, 5'8 Puerto Rican and black dude with hair down his back. He had a slim, 170-pound frame that he kept laced in designer because his older sister was a scam artist at the highest level. People felt like Trey didn't need to hustle because his sister Blanca spoiled him. But Trey wanted his own money and Snatch felt him. GOD bless the child that has his own.

Tasha was a thick, brown-skinned chick from Colony Place who hustled powder to take care of herself and her six kids. Tasha was average in the face, but her body was something out of a magazine. Tasha had a 36,24,52 frame that women went to the doctor to get. Her body was probably why she had six kids and five baby daddies. It was an ongoing joke in the hood that if you touched Tasha, she would get pregnant. But the crazy thing was she'd never fucked with anybody from the hood. Both Snatch and Demon had tried her, but she always screamed that they were too young. The reason Snatch wanted her as an underboss was because her hustle was legit. She hustled to survive not for the hood fame.

Plus she was born and raised in Colony Place. Everyone in the hood knew and fucked with her including all the fiens. Lil Buck was the wild card. Buck was a short 5'5 and black as hell with shoulder-length locks. Buck was is only seventeen and wild as hell. He stayed in some shit because he didn't bite his tongue period! Whateva came to his mind, he said. Buck didn't have any filter. He was brutally honest. But his hustle was second to none! Lil Buck could sell holy water to the devil. His wordplay was crazy; he was one of them ugly niggas with the gift of gab.

"Boy, whatchu got us out here in this hot ass sun for?" Tasha questioned using her hand to fan herself.

"As soon as Action get here, I'll let y'all know what the deal is. Trust me, this is something you don't want to miss" Snatch said.

Action walked up with Alayna strolling behind her, causing Snatch to double-take.

"What she doin' here?" Snatch wanted to know.

"She good, she wit me" Action spoke up.

Snatch wanted to tell Action that Alayna wasn't good but he didn't want to undermine her authority in front of everybody.

"Okay, here's the deal. All y'all is hustleholics and I'm putting together a team of loyal hustlers and money getters called Count Up Boys, CUB gang for short."

"Or Count Up Bitchs" Action chimed in.

"But instead of crack and powder, we're gonna sell boy. It's going way faster than coke and we're going to give it to you at a price where you'll double your money every re-up. And with us bein a unit, your beef is our beef and we have that's gonna handle all of our dirty work willingly," Snatch said with conviction.

"I'm down" Buck instantly said.

"Me too" added Tasha.

"If I can double my money every flip, then I'm down with the program," Zay said.

"What about you?" Demon asked Trey.

"I don't know; I'm really straight with my whole little setup that I got going right now. If it ain't broke, why fix it?"

"You could ger rich quicker than what you're doing now. And just because it ain't broke don't men you can't upgrade it" Demon offered his opinion.

"Slow money better than no money," Trey said.

"That's on you lil bra but know that any hood that's got our stamp on it you won't be allowed to hustle in," Snatch told him.

"Hmph" Trey snorted in disbelief and walked off.

"Fuck him, he'll realize his mistake soon enough," Snatch said ready to go fuck Action.

Action was looking good as hell. She had two French braids in her hair and her lashes and brows were done making Action look edible. The sun had her skin tan and healthy-looking.

"Here's an ounce on the house to get y'all started. For right now, everyone's gonna hustle in Colony Place. We're going to get this hood turned up then branch out. Zay, when we branch out, Massey Hill is gonna be yours. Buck, you goin have Meadowwood and the Strickland Bridge area, and Tasha, Colony Place is yours" Action told them the plan.

"And what is the price goin' to be that's gonna ensure we double our money?" Tasha questioned, thinking that she'd be a millionaire and be able to retire soon.

"Seventy thousand a brick. We were selling ten dollars a point but with us having the best dope we're going to twenty a point which equals up to two hundred a gram, fifty-six hundred an ounce and two hundred a bird," Demon stated.

"Count Up!" Buck yelled.

"I'm about to hit up the block" Tasha cuffed her ounce and strutted off.

"She got the right idea," Zay said putting his ounce in his shorts.

"That all?" asked Buck.

"Yea, hire y'all some workers to take some of the workloads off of you. Trust me, you're gonna need some good help" Snatch said.

"That went well, Action said as they walked off.

"Action, Alayna isn't to be around any kind of illegal shit. What if Trey would have got on that crazy shit and guns got drawn?" Snatch gave her his reasoning.

"You can't tell me what to do, Alayna said and walked away on her phone.

"What up Snatch?' Rambo walked up.

"I'm glad you walked up. From now on, anybody that ain't with us can't get money over here. If you catch em hustling, you can do whatever you deem fit. Your goanna be our security. Put you a squad together and y'all gon get rich. Make sure your entire squad is like you" Snatch put him on. "And the next time you see that nigga Trey, put his brains on the pavement" he handed Rambo twenty bands.

"Done deal" Rambo pocketed the money.

"We been bullshitin' enough, it's time to get to this paper," Demon urged.

They walked deeper into the hood and got their hustle on putting the groundwork down to setting their plan in motion.

Chapter 12

They moved the entire fifteen bricks in ten days! Colony Place was a million-dollar trap now. Fiens were coming from all over to cop the potent heroin. There was a line of cars leading all the way out to Owen Drive, the flow was nonstop.

"We on the way to the top my nigga," Demon said.

"That's definitely the way it's looking," Snatch said as he looked down into the parking lot.

Snatch, Action, and Demon were on the roof of one of the buildings smoking, looking down at all the traffic flow.

"Once we snatch up them, other hoods shit gonna be crazy, we cleared over two million in less than two weeks! What do you think we gon do once we have the entire city copping from us?" Action now saw Snatch's vision but on a small scale.

"The City? Let's try the state," Snatch vowed.

If heroin is as pure as they were getting it? No one in the U.S. was going to be able to compete with them on any level.

"And I just ordered some stamps for us to stamp our bags with. Since we reppin' C.U.B. gang and a CUB is a baby bear, I got pictures of baby bears on the stamps. That's gon' be our signature," said Demon taking a pull of the potent weed Action had rolled up.

"I like that," Action grinned

"I went to Snatch Massey Hill up first since it's so close to us. Really, we ain't gotta Snatch it, we just goin' put Zay over there and be out there with him for a few days. Because don't nobody really run Massey Hill. So once Zay posts up with his team, niggas is goin' fall in line." Snatch coughed after pulling on the Za-filled Dutchmaster.

"We gon start that tomorrow and then this weekend, we gon set Buck up on Meadowwood," Action stated.

"Ain't that nigga Trey right there?" Demon pointed at a dude sitting on a grey Audi. Snatch looked and sure enough, Trey was sitting in the parking lot selling work.

"Oh, he thinks this shit a game" Snatch looked on as Trey made play after play.

"Uh oh," said Action.

Rambo walked up to Trey and said something to Trey that made him get up off of the car he was sitting on. Rambo stepped up on him and sat him back down in the car with a bullet under his chin. They could see the red mist explode out of the top of Trey's head from the rooftop. Snatch looked at Action and Demon and smirked. The first example has been made.

"Impressive. I really wasn't expecting to see you again for at least another month" Yuki said.

"Get used to seeing me on the regular. This is the come-up that I been dreamin' about for a while. So I'm gonna make the most of it and milk it until it runs dry.

"Trust me, it won't run dry, EVER" Yuki bragged.

"You know what they say, nothing lasts forever. All things must come to an end" Snatch vowed.

"Not this one," Yuki responded not reading between the lines and picking up on the warning in Snatch's words.

"There's six-fifty in the bag. That covers the first five and twenty more."

Yuki nodded his head. "Take one-twenty-five out, that's yours. Consider it a little bonus on the side," he said as he grabbed his phone.

Yuki said something in rapid Chinese and hung up. "They'll be in your trunk." he got up, concluding their meeting.

Snatch sat there a while after Yuki left trying to get his thoughts in order.

"What you doin Sumajee," Ming Li asked as she came and sat down at the table with Snatch.

"Chillin', Thinkin.' Whatcho pretty ass got going on?" He openly admired her.

" Nothin, about to go home" she smiled.

"You gon take me home with you?" she smiled.

"You do not want to go to me house, Alayna would kill you. And my boyfriend get mad.

"Ain't nobody thinking about Alayna or your boyfriend. I do what I want when I want" Snatch bossed up.

"Didn't mean to offend you" she said meekly looking down.

Snatch stood up and walked to Ming Li. He put his hand under her chin and tilted it up until she was looking for him in the eyes.

"You can't offend me with words Ming." Snatch moved a strand of hair out of her face.

"Walk me to car," she said and smiled.

"I thought you worked at the nail salon?" Snatch walked with her out into the scorching hot sun. Snatch's shirt instantly started sticking to him. "Me do. I come here to look over things for mother sometimes" Ming Li put on a pair of Gucci shades.

Ming Li was a bad, bougie little bitch. Everything about her was prissy as hell. She had high maintenance.

"What?" she looked at Snatch over the top of her shades.

"Yo little ass is too funny" Snatch smiled opening her car door for her.

"Are you ridin' with me to house?" Ming Li sat down in her Lexus Coupe giving Snatch a good view between her legs.

Her pussy looked like it was trying to bust out of the seams of the yellow short set she had on. "Stop it," she said closing her legs when she saw where he had his eyes trained.

Snatch couldn't figure Ming Li's vibes out. One minute she was acting as if she was flirting with him and the next, she was somewhat cold. He wondered did she know that if he comes to her house, he had plans on fucking her little brains out.

"Oh shit! I gotta go baby girl, I got something I need to handle" he walked off towards his car. Snatch had forgotten all about the work. He got to his old school and popped the trunk. There were way more than the twenty bricks he'd paid for.

"Yuki, you got all the sense," Snatch said out loud and closed the trunk.

"Are you okay sir?" a detective asked.

Snatch was already sweating but now his whole body was sweating.

"I'm good" Snatch took the cop in.

The detective was a middle-aged, block dude with a brush out. He looked like he had spent too many shifts at the donut shop. He was about thirty pounds too heavy to chase Snatch if he took off running. Snatch looked around and saw that he was by himself, putting an end to the thought of running. If he got overzealous, Snatch was going to make the city fly the flag half-staff for their fallen comrade.

"Okay, well, have a good day sir" he walked off to his black Mustang convertible with the light brown soft top.

Snatch got in his car and dropped the dope off to Action. He'd been right, Yuki had put extra twenty bricks in the trunk.

"Mike, that kid looks real familiar," Detective Holf said and got behind the wheel of his Mustang and watched Snatch ride off.

"What, is he a troublemaker?" His partner questioned.

"Nah, it's not that." Holt raked his brain trying to put his finger on where he knew the boy from. "I'll be damned," he slapped him across the face.

He sped off towards the police station; he had to check his lunch out because if he was correct, then he had some things to look into.

Chapter 13

They set Zay up in Massey Hill without a problem. Zay put a spot-on Southern Ave. and one in Stanton Arms to try and combat all the traffic the potent dope was going to bring but it was no use. There were still cars lined up at both spots. Anybody that knew nasty Massey knew that it was already hot, but traffic flowed like that was gonna have the Jones running down something serious.

"Zay, we know that it's only a matter of time before shit gets hot but we don't want it to get hot ASAP. Go ahead and open up three more spots because this is why too much traffic." Snatch stood on the porch of the spot-on Southern Avenue. " See, in Colony Place, we gon see the jakes way before they come. Plus, we got lookouts at the entrance but over here, there are so many ways for the jakes to come through that you can't combat it. Once we get the other spots jumpin', the traffic gon subside a little bit"

"Already," Zay said.

Massey Hill or *Nasty Massey* as some called it had always been a get-money spot since back in the day. Massey wasn't nothing but a housing division with some old rundown houses and some okay ones. Highway 301 ran outside of it, so it was always jumping. It had gotten so bad that the city had installed cameras on the light poles. The niggas in the hood weren't going for it though. They shot them out so much that after the twentieth time of coming out to fix them, the city just said to hell with fixing them.

"Jason, what the hell are you doin' out here?" Snatch ran up to him. "Take yo ass home."

"You can't tell me what to do," he mean-mugged Snatch.

"Lil nigga, you got life fucked up! Janice would kill me if I let something happen to you. Take ya ass back to the hood boy before you make me show out," Snatch snapped.

"Big bro, he a spinner, he apart of Dizzy gang" Rambo stepped up.

"A spinner? Dizzy gang? What the fuck is all that?" It was all new to Snatch.

"Nigga, you know what the fuck a spinner is. A nigga that be spinnin' on shit" Zay chimed in.

"Ooh oh," Snatch nodded his head.

"And Dizzy gang is my shit. It's called Dizzy gang because everybody on the team gone spin until they get dizzy. DG nigga" Rambo bragged.

"I'm tryin' to get dizzy right now," Jason said pulling an ARP out of his shorts.

Snatch took a step back and looked at little Jason. Janice's little brother had mentally grown into a man-child. He held the same look in his eyes that Rambo did when he was on his bullshit. The streets had grabbed a hold of Jason. And now it was nothing Snatch could do but try and guide him so he didn't get himself killed before his eighteenth birthday.

"How many niggas you done spun off?" Snatch questioned.

"Five, and three of them man down" Jason boasted.

"Rambo, I'm holding you personally responsible for him. If something happened to him, it's going be your head on a pike," Snatch warned.

"Snatch, I don't have a say in what he does, and for real for real, he gets just as active as I do. I'm not gonna hold his hand trying to watch out for him while it's going down will have me in the dirt. He knows what he's sign up for. Live by the gun, die by the gun" Rambo spoke as if he was a grown man and not a twelve-year-old.

"If I do die by the gun, I'ma die wit an empty clip. You can believe that," Jason said arrogantly.

"I'm telling Janice," Snatch said making everybody laugh but he was dead ass serious.

Snatch was scrolling through his contacts when a call from Demon came through.

"What up nigga?" Snatch answered his phone.

"Boy, I'm down bad! These Murk Mob Niggas got me stuck in Rosemary. They seek me and start bussin' at my whip! I had to hop out my whip and dip to this little shorty house ova here." He was out of breath.

"I'm on the way!" Snatch ended the call. "Y'all niggas wanna spin, come on," he told Jason and Rambo. They hopped in Snatch's new smoke-grey Trackhawk and broke the speed limit getting to Murchison Road.

"Hand me that Draco off the backseat," Snatch urged Jason.

Snatch turned into Rosemary and immediately saw niggas walking around clutching pistols. The tint on the windows prevented them from seeing who was inside the jeep. There was even a nigga in a wheelchair rolling around with an AR15 across his lap.

"Where the hell you at?" Snatch called Demon.

"I'm in the second set of townhouses," he said.

"I'm out here in my jeep" Snatch backed up to the second set of townhouses and waited.

"I thought we were about to spin on something" Jason clutched the ARP, looking out of the tinted windows at the Murk Mob dudes milling about.

"Patience, young grasshopper," Snatch grinned enjoying Jason's urgency.

"Here I come right now," Demon said.

"Come on!" Snatch hopped out bringing his Draco up KAH! KAH!KAH! Snatch's bullets found a home in the face of an unsuspecting Murk Mob member.

CHA!CHA!CHA!CHA! Jason let the ARP bark and duck behind a car then come out letting the ARP bark again before ducking back down killing three of the opps. Not to be outdone, Rambo jumped out of the jeep shooting twin Glock 27s immediately sending two niggas to the afterlife. Rambo cut his eyes at Jason, and they started walking down on shit! Every time their hammers spat, a body would fall. They were so in sync with each other that it looked like they had been trained to kill shit! Secretly, Snatch was impressed but he'd never tell though. After watching them in action, Snatch knew he didn't have to worry about Jason; his pistol play was legit!

Demon came out of the townhouse shooting a choppa. The few remaining Murk Mob niggas took off running seeing their comrades' bodies fall around them at such a rapid pace. They all rushed to the jeep and Snatch got them the hell away from the Murk.

"Bra, something I forgot to tell you that you need to know is that Chance didn't die that night. He was the one who spotted me" Demon told him.

"I didn't see him out there," said Snatch.

"He was in a wheelchair" Demon said.

Chapter 14

"I know it Mine! that's Quiet Storm's son," detective Holt told his partner.

"Who?"

"That kid we saw the other day at the Asian restaurant that I said looked familiar," detective Hold said jubilantly.

"What's so incredible about him being Quiet Storm's son?" he questioned clicking off of Pornhub.

"I'm a firm believer that the apple doesn't fall far from the tree. And both of his parents were hustlers, so there's a very strong possibility that he followed in their footsteps."

Mike had been a rookie fresh out of the police academy when the whole Quiet Storm saga was taking place. Detective Holt had been the lead man on the case until the FEDS swooped in and took over. Detective Holt felt like he was on the verge of bringing Storm down, he even had an informant who was willing to testify on Quiet Storm but the FEDS assumed total control cutting the Fayetteville Police Department all the way out of the equation. To this day, detective Holt wouldn't work with the FEDS. The Quiet Storm bust was the biggest bust in North Caroline to date.

Detective Holt hated drug dealers with a passion because his sister and mother had overdosed when he was young. Most of the force thought that was why he had been obsessed with Quiet Storm down but it wasn't; the real reason was because Quiet Storm had been fucking detective Holt's wife! Detective Hold could remember it like it was yesterday...

"Sabrina!" Detective Holt yelled walking into his house. He hung his jacket and gun on the back of one of the kitchen chairs and walked down the hall. The closer he go to his bedroom, the more he though he heard his wife talking.

"Sabrina?" He said and still didn't receive an answer. Detective Holt got to his bedroom and his heart fell out of his chest to the floor. His wife of ten years was in their bed on all fours getting thrashed by Quiet Storm.

"Stor,! Storm! Fuck your pussy boy!" Detective Holt's wife screamed as Quiet Storm gripped her wide hips.

"Sabrina, what what the hell?" Detective hold stammered. Quiet Storm grabbed his pistol off of the bed beside him and looked at Detective Holt.

"Johnathan? Oh my God, what are you doing home?" Sabrina looked back at her husband standing in the doorway to their bedroom.

She tried to move but Quiet Storm held her in place. Quiet Storm saw the badge on detective Holt's waist and picked up where he left off pounding her out.

"If you move from that spot, you'll get the whole clip," Quiet Storm said releasing inside of Sabrina. Detective Hold watched as Quiet Storm put his clothes on and walked out. Noting in Detective Holt's life was the same after that. His marriage was never the same; he wanted to divorce his wife but they went to counseling and made things right. Detective Holt never fully trusted Sabrina again. He immersed himself in his work and devoted his life to taking Quiet Storm down and ruining his life.

"Johnathan! Johnathan!" Detective Vance snapped him out of his painful flashback

"Do you think he's dealing?" Detective Vance inquired.

"I don't know as of yet but I plan on finding out," he said trying to shake off the memory of his wife in bed with another man.

"Holt! Vance! My office now!" Police Chief Thomas yelled from the door at her office.

"What's going on Chief?" Detective Holt took a seat in her office and grabbed an open bag of cool ranch doritos off her desk and started eating them.

Detective Vance opted to stand up. Detective Holt and Chief Thomas were golf buddies, so they had a better relationship than everyone at the station and they were both black.

"I need you guys to go to Colony Place and see what's going on. We've been receiving complaints of a lot of traffic and drug activity. Chief Thomas said grudgingly.

Chief Alicia Thomas was always in a sour mood; she had been on the force for the last twenty-two years, the last ten as Police Chief. Chief Thomas joined the force straight out of high school at the age of eighteen. She made her way up the ladder being a hard-nosed cop. Chief Thomas was a pretty, chocolate-skinned stallion. She felt she needed to go above and beyond because of her looks and skin tone. During her first seven years on the force, she led the department in arrests and drugs seized. Chief Thomas was Fayetteville's first Black Police Chief and the first-ever female Chief.

"Hey Chied, do you remember the Quiet Storm case?" Detective Holt questioned.

"Of course, why do you ask?'" she raised her brow

"Because we ran across his son the other day and I want to check him out. His bloodline is tainted, and I can almost guarantee he's followed in his fathers' footsteps. Their resemblance is uncanny" Detective Hold reached.

"Johnathan, what is that little boy, seventeen? Leave it alone detective, that's an order," she warned

Chief Thomas was one of the only people who knew about the personal beef that detective Holt had against Quiet Storm.

"Okay, okay" he put his hands up in surrender.

"Now, y'all go and check out those Colony Place complaints" Chief Thomas rushed them out of her office.

"So are you gonna let it go?" Questioned Detective Vance once they got to the car.

"Can you fly?"

They drove to Colony Place bit. Once they got across the bridge on Owen drive, they saw a line of cars extending out of the neighborhood.

"Is there an accident up ahead?" Detective Holt strained his eyes to see.

"Not that I can see" Detective Vance responded.

Detective Holt flashed the blue lights on the mustang causing the line of cars to dissipate. They were able to drive into the neighborhood without any delay once the cars left.

"That's weird, what was holding them up?" Detective Vance didn't see anything out of the ordinary as they drove through Holiday Park and down into Colony Place.

"I think we fucked up by flashing the lights" detective Holt stated watching everyone watch the tinted Mustang as they rode through.

He couldn't have been more correct. The minute he flashed the blue lights, the lookouts radioed that an undercover was coming and everything stopped. None of the workers made a slam, they all just watched the tinted-out Mustang drive through. All the apartments that held large quantities of dope in them were waiting on the word on whether or not to dump the heroin in the large vats that had sulfuric acid. The acid would eat the dope leaving no trace of it. Snatch wasn't going to allow anyone to get caught with a large quantity of dope thus eliminating the risk of someone telling him. He didn't even allow Demon to handle large amounts, it was really pointless because him, Demon and Action were busting all the profits down. This way, Snatch was the one taking all the risks. Then some of the apartments had walls knocked out of them connecting two or more apartments together.

Detective Holt looked Colony Place over as they passed through and didn't see anything that would give him the idea that there was anything illegal going on. Then his eyes landed on Snatch sitting on top of one of the buildings, smoking a blunt watching his car ride past.

"We need to switch cars and ride back through," Detective Holt said to his partner.

"Let's do it."

They waited an hour, got in detective Holt's green chevy Tahoe and rode back through. This time, the detectives were able to see colony place for what it was—a dope boy paradise. Not only were there lines of cars waiting to get served but there were junkies on foot getting their fix.

"Zombie land" detective Vance mumbled looking out of the window.

Detective Holt's eyes were fixated on Snatch as he watched the activity. Detective Holt watched as numerous people walked up to Snatch and talked with him. He was praying that Snatch gave someone some drugs while he was watching but he didn't. Detective Holt took in Snatch's posture, his air, the way he was moving, and a light bulb went in his head; like father, like son.

"Look at the way everyone interacts with him. He's the boss; this is his show." Detective Holt took his iPhone out and recorded all the activities particularly Snatch's.

He wanted to show Chief Thomas what he saw. He needed her to give him the okay to start an investigation into Mr. Sunajee Brooks. He wanted to send Snatch to live with his father in the penitentiary.

Chapter 15

Chance being alive was a minor problem in Snatch's eyes; plus he was in a wheelchair. If anything, this was going to allow Snatch to hold his nuts on Chance the way Chance had done him in the club that night.

"Are you still thinking about Chance still being alive?" Action questioned watching him look out of her bedroom window over Colony Place.

"Nah." He lied.

"You're such a liar," Action said as she walked up behind him and wrapped her arms around his waist.

Action was horny and wanted some dick. Action turned Snatch around by his waist and dropped to her knees. She unbuckled his Gucci belt and undid his shorts causing them to fall around his ankles. Snatch looked down at Action as she pulled his swollen manhood out of his boxers. Snatch bit down on his bottom lip as Action stroked his dick. Snatch put his hand on the back of her head and guided her head towards his dick. He was finally going to see what Action's head game was hitting on.

"Boy boo," she said when Snatch's dick got to her lips. Action stood up still gripping Snatch's pole and led him to her bed. Action pushed him back on the bed and began to take her clothes off. She pulled her tank top over her head freeing her succulent C cups.

"Let your hair down," Snatch said huskily while stroking his dick up and down.

Action took the scrunchie holding her bag, blond hair in a ponytail out allowing her hair to fall, framing her pretty face. Action then unbuttoned the jean shorts she was wearing and shimmed them down her shapely legs leaving her standing in a white G-string. Action straddled Snatch's body locking his pole between her legs.

"Still thinking about Chance?" she grinned putting one of her breasts to his lips.

Snatch sucked her nipple into his mouth causing her to emit a cry of passion.

"SSS!" Action bit her lip as electric currents ran through her body.

Snatch continued sucking her breast and toyed with her clit through her G-string. Action reached between her legs, pulled her G-string to the side and maneuvered her body so that Snatch's dick entered her velvety folds.

"Fuck!" they said in unison.

Snatch leaned back on the bed and Action started rocking her hips in a forward motion as if she was riding one of those mechanical bulls.

"Mmmm!" ride this dick!"

Snatch slapped her on the ass leaving a red handprint on her butt. Action put both of her hands on Snatch's chest and began to jerk her hips.

"Just like that," Snatch coached her.

"I'm cumin!' Action yelled falling onto his chest.

Snatch held her hips and stroked up into her center making Action bite his shoulder.

"Damn, what's goin' on here?" Demon asked as he walked in the room. Demon snatched his shirt off and walked behind Action. He pulled her G-string out of her ass, spat in the crack of her ass and rubbed it in. Demon pulled his already hard wood and lined it up with her backdoor. Action looked back over her shoulder at Demon to see what he was doing. Then she used her hands to spread her cheeks apart.

Demon entered Actions butt slowly allowing her time to adjust to his intrusion.

"Oh shit! Yea! Yea! Yea!" Action screamed in ecstasy from Demon and Snatch filling both of her holes. Snatch and Demon found a rhythm and drug Action. Demon filled Actions butt with his kids followed shortly by Snatch unloading inside of her love box.

"Damn!" Demon said going to the bathroom to clean up. Action rolled off of Snatch and laid there while Snatch fixed his clothes.

"I love the shit out of y'all" Action admitted.

"You know it's all love" Snatch replied checking his iPhone.

"Okey den! Count up Buck!" Snatch yelled.

"What are you yellin' about?' Demon walked back in the room.

"Lil Buck set himself up in Meadowwood. He just sent me a text sayin' that he got a spot in Meadowwood, Robinwood, Creeks Edge and Shanaondoah, thus givin' us control of the Strickland Bridge area. He said niggas was cool with the move since everybody gon get rich," Snatch told them the good news.

"This shit too easy but you do know that takin' ova the Murk is a dead issue with Chance bein alive," Demon reminded Snatch.

"Not necessarily. A king only holds his position if he keeps his soldiers and his people happy. You don't think it's a nigga on the Murk that wants that top spot. Before we put him in that wheelchair, he was tall, stocky and had them long-ass dreadlocks, but now, he skinny as hell; his brown-skin looks pale and his locks look raggedy as fuck! His time is comin', trust me. We gon keep strengthening our hold on the city and grab up the hoods around the Murk. And something else I want y'all to do and do it ASAP, move out of the hood, treat yourselves; we deserve it. And Action, tell

Tasha she gotta come up with a solution to all the car traffic; it's too much," Snatch said and left.

"Boy, where are you takin' me?" Snatch's mom asked.

"Yea, because I'm ready to take this blindfold off" Alayna complained.

"Y'all so impatient, just relax and chill out dang!" Snatch smiled.

Snatch parked his jeep and got out. He walked around to his mom's side and opened the passenger side door helping her out of the Track hawk then helped Alayna out.

"Okay y'all can take the blindfolds off."

"Oh my God! Whose house is this? His mom stared.

"Ma stop playin with me. You know this is yours and I put it in your name, so can't nobody take it from you, it's all yours" Snatch said bringing tears to her eyes.

Snatch bought his mom a six-bedroom, three-bath, four-cat garage mansion in a gated community. In his eyes, she deserved it.

"Whatchu get me?" Alayna's spoiled ass whined.

"You know I couldn't forget about my other baby," he smiled

Snatch hit the garage door opener and it slid up revealing a pink 2023 Porsche 911 GT3 and a dark blue 2023 Bentley Bentayga.

"Which one is mine?" Alayna dashed to the garage

"The Porsche and the Bentley is mama's"

"Thank you, son," she hugged Snatch's neck and went to go check her new home out. It felt good to put a smile on his mom's face. Now it was time for him to go have a little fun. Snatch wasn't going to go crazy on himself, yet he was going to wait until he flipped his re-up three more times, then he was going to snap! But he had brought himself a new wardrobe and a nice two-story house in a quiet neighborhood in Hope Mills away from the city. He'd been all work no play but tonight was playtime. Snatch went home, got in the shower and got dressed for the night. He opted to wear some black Chanel shorts, a black Chanel shirt with Chanel written across the front in white and some black and white Chanel sneakers. Snatch had brought a big-face Rolex and gotten it bust down. He put that on and his three-inch-thick Cuban link, he left it at that because he didn't want to be too flashy. Snatch grabbed his .40 with the thirty and thirty racks and hopped in the track hawk. He pulled up to Pandora's sports bar twenty minutes later and walked in. He walked straight to the third floor and asked for D-One.

"What up big time?" D-One asked coming out of the door.

"Big time?" "Nah, I'm small fish" Snatch handed him the five bands for the month-long VIP pass. D-One handed him a card and walked with him onto the third floor.

"I'm gon pull up on you a little later, enjoy yourself," D-One said and walked off.

Now Snatch saw what was so exclusive about the third floor. Whereas the other two floors were a sports bar with a club feel, the third floor had a club/strip feel. The waitresses up here barely had on any clothes and the bottle girls only wore ping g-strings. Unlike the other two floors, the third floor didn't have a bar in the middle, the elevated bar was against the wall with TVs all around it. There were five VIP areas that sat above the floor looking down on everyone else. One of the areas was empty, so Snatch made his way towards it.

"It's gon cost you five hundred" a bottle girl said seeing where Snatch was headed.

Snatch peeled off five bills and handed them to her.

"Bring me a bottle of Ciric." Snatch paid her for the bottle and tipped her a bill.

"Big Time, I see you doing big things," D-One sais as he walked up the steps to the booth.

"Why do you keep callin' me big time?" Snatch wanted to know.

"Snatch, it ain't too much that go in the city that I don't know about. You're on the come-up. You and your crew are on a historic tear. Colony Place, Nasty Massey, Strickland Bridge area." D-One let him know he wasn't just talking out of the side of his neck.

"I think you got the wrong guy," Snatch played dumb.

"I like that. Humbleness, keep it up and you'll last a long time. Most eighteen-year-olds would've beat their chest braggin' and boastin'. It's clear you're in it for the dough and not the fame. I like your style little Quiet Storm. I actually wanna pull your coat tail to some things" D-One said sincerely.

Snatch looked at him waiting on him to continue. D-One grinned and continued. "That dope you have is gon to take you above and beyond but......you're about to make a lot of enemies. Always remember, jealousy breeds envy, envy spawns hate. Your foundation is solid, but you need to tighten a few things up. First, you need to go pay you a lawyer, not just any lawyer but the best one in the city. Then pay you a bondsman in advance in case you get locked up and can't get to your money."

"Why are you tellin' me all of this?"

"Because you have the makin' of bein something special plus your pops did some real nigga shit back in the day. Something else that would be wise of you to do is get you a dirty cop on your payroll to feed you information. And I understand that you fully trust you team as you should but keep some things to yourself." D-One stood up. "That's your hood lesson for the day. Digest all of that and come holla at me" he walked down the steps.

Snatch wondered why the OG was really giving him the game. He knew a whole lot about Snatch and what he had going on, yet Snatch knew nothing about him. But he knew how to fix that.

Chapter 16

The next day, Snatch went downtown to talk to a bail bondsman by the name of Amanda.
"What exactly can I do for you?" she inquired.
Amanda was an older white lady in her mid to late forties. She was skinny with strawberry blond hair; she looked vaguely familiar but Snatch didn't know from where.
"I'm trying to make you my personal bondsman. I wanna pay you in advance in case me or my people get locked up." Snatch got right down to business.
"Umm….okay" she scratched her arm and that's when it came to Snatch where he'd seen her before; she loved Percocets. Snatch had run across a hundred perks one time and someone had referred her to him because he didn't know anybody who did them.
"Amanda, you don't remember me?" Snatch questioned and she shook her head. "You brought those hundred perks from me that time."
"Yea" her eyes brightened. "What do you have going on trying to pay in advance for a bond? You don't think you jinxing yourself?"
"Not really, I'm preparing myself just in case."
"Okay, I got you' she shrugged.
Snatch went out to his jeep and grabbed a duffel bag. She looked inside and her eyes got big as saucers.
"How much is this?"
"A million."

"What?!"

"Yea, so if any of my people or me get locked up, it won't be an issue for you to come get us. Let me know if you can't handle this and I'll go somewhere else," Santch said while he looked her in the eyes.

"No, no, no. it's just no one's ever done this before. It's actually a smart move. You have no idea how many people call me every day from jail trying to get me to come bail them out on the promise that they'll get me my money once they get out," she informed him.

They shook hands and Snatch left out. He sat in his Trackhawk for a minute thinking, then went back inside. "Amanda, I don't need to tell you the outcome if you play me" he warned. "No, you don't. I don't have a reason to," she reassured him.

Snatch walked back out and drove down the street to the law offices of D. W. Kray. He was the best lawyer in Fayetteville followed by James Parish. Kray hadn't lost a trial in the last five years and Parish was twenty and four in the past five years, so they were the best of the best. Kray was a forty-something-year-old white dude with a low cut. He kinda looked like the actor Matthew Mc Conoughey who played the lawyer in the movie, A Time To Kill. What Snatch liked the most about Kray was his dress code. All his suits were perfectly tailored and designer and his arrogance was reassuring.

"Hi, how may I help you?" the secretary greeted when Snatch walked in.

"I'm here to see Mr. Kray" Snatch looked around the office at the many pictures adoring the walls of Kray posing with famous people.

"Do you have an appointment sir?"

"No"

"Well, you have to set up an --------" she didn't get to finish her sentence because Snatch walked past her desk into Kray's office.

"Sorry sir, he just barged in. do you want me to call the police?" She questioned.

Kray looked up from his desk at his secretary then at Snatch and said "no Sarah, it's okay. Have a seat Mr…"

"Brooks, Sumajee Brooks" Snatch took a seat.

"What can I do for you?"

"I want to hire you in advance. I don't currently have any pending charges but I mean to be prepared just in case I do." Sarah hoped he could read between the lines.

"What kind of case do you suspect you may catch if you don't mind me asking?"

"A drug case."

"Oh, that's nothing. There's a five-thousand-dollar retainer fee and I charge a hundred dollars an hour for drug cases and two hundred and fifty an hour for murders."

"So that twenty-four hundred a day" Snatch did the math in his head, got up and headed to his jeep. Snatch walked back into Mr. Kray's office and dropped a duffel bag on his desk.

"There is a million dollars in the bag, that should cover any and all of your fees for whatever case I may catch Mr Kray" Snatch said smugly.

"Call me Daniel." He swiped the duffel bag behind his desk and reached over to shake Snatch's hand." You said your name is Sumajee Brooks. You wouldn't by chance be related to Stanley Brooks?'

"That's my dad. Why you ask?"

"The resemblance. Here's my personal number, if by chance you get arrested call me. Don't say a word."

"Okay," Snatch walked out and was almost to his jeep when he heard a gun cock. Snatch slowly turned around and saw Chance in the passenger seat of a black challenger.

"You bitch ass niggas paralyzed me from the waist down. Payback is a motherfucks" Chance aimed a cannon at Snatch. Snatch dove beside his jeep. Soon as he hit the ground, Snatch was up and running! BOOM! BOOM!

BOOM! TAT! TAT!TAT!TAT! Chance and somebody else were trying to take Snatch out of the game. He could hear the bullets whizzing by his head as he ran. Snatch pulled his Springfield .40 off his hip and shot blindly over his shoulders as he ran. He hopped a fence and came out on the next street.

"Fuck!" Snatch bent over out of breath.

He started walking down the street when the black challenger Chance was in, a blue mustang and two red chargers bent the corner busting. Snatch sent a few rounds their way when a bullet hit the .40 knocking it out of his hand. He took off running again. Snatch jumped another fence and came out on Old Wilmington Road. No sooner than he got on the street, one of the chargers hit the corner spraying KAH! KAH! KAD! Two Murk Mob Niggas sent 7062's his way from their choppas. Snatch was tired as hell! He ran down a side street and right into a parked police cruiser.

"What are you running from?" the cop got out of his cruiser.

Snatch was so out of breath he couldn't answer but he knew he was safe now. The blue mustang turned on the side street and gunned it in Snatch's direction.

"What the hell?" the cop reached for his pistol.

TAT!TAT!TAT! they gunned the cop down before his pistol could clear the holster. Snatch knew he had to get somewhere safe because they weren't going to stop until they killed him. He climbed the fence and entered the Old Cambell Terrance now called Oak Run.

"Snatch! Oh My God, you're bleedin'!" Sasha rushed up to him.

"Where your car at?" He asked out of breath.

"Come on" she led him to a white Dodge Demon. "What is going on?"

"Just get me to my whip" Snatch had caught his breath. Sasha pulled out and passed the white challenger on the way out of the apartment complex. Snatch survived an all-out assassination attempt on his life. He now knew he had to go ahead and crush Chance totally or his cripple ass was going to get lucky and kill Snatch.

Chapter 17

"They got shit fucked up!" Demon rasped pacing back and forth.

"Hurry up so I can go get dizzy" Rambo urges.

" Boy, go sit down before I call yo momma" Evette warned finishing up on Snatch's hand.

They were at Demon's mom's house letting her stitch his hand up where a bullet had put a deep gash in it.

"Are you gonna tell me what happened now?" Sasha questioned Snatch.

"Why you ain't done yet? I don't know why you followed me here anyway." Snatch looked at her trying to avoid looking at the stitches being put in his hand.

"That pussy nigga Chance tried to kill my boy." Action was ready to get active as well.

"You talking about Chance from the Murk?" Sasha asked.

"Yea, that guy," Demon continued to pace.

"You owe me nigga and I plan on collecting too," Sasha glared at Snatch. "I know where his mom, his sister, him and all three of his son's mama's stay at," she offered.

"Hoe, do you know all of this?" Rambo looked at her.

"About four months ago, Chance was tryin' to holla at me and he's the braggin' type. So, he showed me all of their houses talkin' about he paid all of their bills and he would do the same for me," Sasha told Chance's business.

"Where does his mama stay at?" Snatch's face darkened.

"Gates Four. She stays in the very back in the last house on the left. His sister has a house in Aaron Lakes, it's a big blue house that sits on the lake. One of his baby mamas stays in West Point. As soon as you turn in, make a left and go around the curve. Her house sits right on the corner. She drives a purple BMW. The other two both stay on the westside in Foxfire. It's gon be a white Escalade with thirties in her yard and the other one parks her yellow Camaro by the front door. Then his dusty ass stays in Gates Four too right next door to his mama. His extra ass always got that re Porsche in the driveway."

"Let's ride," Snatch stood up.

"I'm not gonna tell you not to go, just be careful" Demon's mom put a hand on his forearm.

"Call me after you take care of your business," Sasha said once they got outside.

Snatch just nodded his head, he was on demon time. He'd been so close to death a few hours ago; he could still feel the grim reaper breathing on the back of his neck.

"Where to first bra?" Action questioned Snatch.

"His mama's house."

Snatch, Action and Jason got in Snatch's Trackhawk and Demon and Rambo got in Demon's brand new shadow black Cadillac Escalade. Jason hadn't said two words the entire time they'd been at Demon's mom's house. Gucci's man downplayed softly while they rode to Gates Four, an upper-class housing division. The whole ride, no one uttered one word. They followed Sasha's instructions to Chance's mom's house noticing the red Porsche in the driveway next door. It was ten thirty at night and there were lights on in both houses, which was a good thing in Snatch's eyes.

"Which one first?" Rambo's thirst for blood evident.

Snatch started walking towards Chance's house. They hadn't discussed a game plan and he didn't feel like they needed to. Him, Action, Demon and Rambo had been putting work in together, so he wasn't worried about anything going wrong. Snatch peeked in Chance's window and saw Chance, his three sons, a Murk Mob dude and some chick sitting in the living room.

"Demon, kick the door in," Snatch said.

Demon kicked the door in, and Snatch rushed in firing! He caught the Murk Mob dud in the chest with three slugs from him taking him off his feet. Action smartly rushed over and kicked Chance in the chest knocking him out of his wheelchair. Rambo sent the chick to meet her maker with a dome shot. Chance's sons all huddled around him. They ranged in ages six to ten.

"I thought you had died that night after pandora's. You shoulda kept it that way because mow tonight is your last night on this earth." Snatch said with conviction.

"But you won't be going by yourself. We're gonna make this a family affair" Demon said suggestively.

"Fuck you pussies! I don't fear shit, particularly your young fuck boys" Chance spat pushing himself up into a sitting position.

Action smiled, "You ain't gotta fear us but you're gonna wish you had real soon. Rambo, y'all go next door and bring his mama over here."

"While we wait though, let me give you something to think about," Demon flashed a demonic grin.

Demon snatched the six-year-old up, snapped his neck and threw his limp body at Chance. Chance let out a wail seeing his son's lifeless body. Snatch and Action didn't bat an eye; they had seen Demon when he got on his demonic shit. And the faraway look on Demon's face let them know he was on real demon time. Demon didn't play the radio when it came to Snatch, he loved him like a brother, so Chance and the Murk Mob had unleashed the beast coming at Snatch the way they had.

"When I'm done, your bloodline will be a distant memory" Demon rasped.

"Here she is" Jason pushed Chance's mother into the house. She fell onto her knees by Chance.

"What's going on?" she wailed.

"Your son has a debt to pay and we're collecting," Action smirked.

"What does he owe?" she looked up.

"Life," Rambo said and shot her in the face spraying Chance and his two remaining sons with blood and brain matter.

BOC! BOC! Demon shot Chance's other son in both of his legs sending him crashing to the floor crying.

"Shut your ass up!" Demon shot him in the throat silencing him.

"Rrr!" Chance growled in anger, but there was nothing he could do but watch.

"What did yo helpless ass think was goin' to happen? Did you think you had any wins? You mighta had a chance if yo legs worked but…" Snatch looked down on him. "Leave my daddy alone!" The oldest boy yelled at Snatch standing in front of Chance.

"Shut your bitch ass up!" Demon kicked the boy in the chest, sending him tumbling across the room. Before he could get up, Demon was on him. Demon started stomping him like he was a grown man! Demon stomped him until he stopped moving then he drew his leg back and football kicked his head making it turn in an unnatural angle.

"And this all started because you wanted to stunt in the club in front of some hoes" Snatch shook hi head. "Tie him up," he told Jason and Rambo

"Oh, and just to let you know, I'll be payin' you sister a visit tonight too," Demon told Chance.

"Put him in the back of Demon's truck."

They drove to the Murk and parked at the corner of Murk and Slater Avenue.

"Get his bitch ass out" Snatch had something special in the works for Chance. Snatch was about to send a message to the entire Murk Mob and the City that CUB gang wasn't to be fucked with. Snatch slung the rope he had over the stop light.

"Bring him her, hurry up!"

Chance's hands were tied behind his back. Snatch fastened a noose around his neck.

"Wait, wait!" Action ran to the jeep and came back with a spray can and wrote CUB gang on his shirt. Snatch hoisted him up and tied the rope off. They watched as the noose suffocated Chance. Rambo and Jason pulled their ARPs out and filled Chance's body with bullets. Another example has been sent. Leave CUB gang the fuck alone or die a gruesome death.

Chapter 18

"Where do you think we're at, Mexico?" Detective Holt asked.

"Do we have any active cartels in Fayetteville?" Detective Vance inquired.

The detectives were on Murchison Road watching the crime scene techs take pictures of Chance swinging from the red light.

"This is totally unacceptable! Not in my city!" Chief Thomas walked up. "And the hell is CUB gang?! Why the hell hasn't he been cut down? Get the press out of here!" she continued to scream.

"Chief, you need to calm down," Detective Holt said.

"Calm down! It's election year and I'm trying to retain my position, are you nuts?" she fumed. "What can you tell me about this?"

"That's Kavon Short, aka Chance, the leader of the infamous Murk Mob and a thorn in our side for the past six years. He was responsible for most of the drugs sold in the city, at least he was." Detective Holt looked up at Chance's body.

"But it seems that he ran afoul of someone. Not the drug trade in the city is up for grabs or maybe that's what this is all about" Detective Vance gave his input.

"Holy shit! Could this be a power grab by Sumajee?" You see what he had going on in Colony Place. With Chance out of the way, the city drug trade would be his for the taking," Detective Holt grasped at straws.

"Sumajee? Who is that and why don't I have a report on him?" Chief Thomas questioned.

"That's Quiet Storm's son. I showed you the video of him in Colony Place" Detective Holt reminded her.

"I thought I told you to leave him alone? All I saw in that video was a boy talking to a bunch of people. There was nothing of merit in the video concerning him. Johnathan, find out who this CUB gang is. Find out who's running Colony Place and leave Quiet Storm's son alone until you get some cold hard evidence against him. And somebody get this damn boy down!" she stormed off.

"Jeez, her ass is huge" Detective Vance lusted over the Chief's full figure.

Detective Holt pulled his phone out, he needed to talk to some of his informants because his gut instinct was telling him that Sumajee was running the show.

After the demonstration they put downtown Chance, the whole city knew that the Count Up Boys were to be feared and respected. And the dizzy gang was making their presence known! They put the city on notice. Rambo and Jason put a demonstration down so mean on a group of niggas from the westside that the few who survived moved out of town. They caught them in the Cross Creek Mall and shot a hundred rounds! It was on the news for the three days straight! In the wake of all the gunplay, Snatch was able to secure a few more hoods.

Snatch, Demon and Action met with Ray Nate, a dude from Shaw road and put him down with CUB Gang. Then Trigga Tone and SK from Rambo Street got with the program and started copping work from CUB Gang. And once Los found out the prices CUB gang was blessing people with, he quickly jumped on board giving CUB gang control of downtown as well. They had succeeded in grabbing all the hoods surrounding the Murk. Snatch was slowly working his way around the city continuing to implement his plan. Something Snatch had noticed lately was that there had been a lot of 14K members out and about. He'd been seeing them way more than he usually did. Snatch pulled into Exclusive Nails and saw Alayna's pink Porsche in the parking lot. He grabbed two duffel bags off the backseat of the Trackhawk and walked inside.

"Hey Sumajee" Ming Li shrieked when he walked in and he nodded his head.

"Wassup big bro" Alayna looked up from Ming Li doing her nails.

"Sup Sissy?" he kissed her on the cheek and continued to the back.

Snatch was here on business; he would talk to her on the way out.

"What's going on Yuki?" They shook hands and Snatch took a seat in the office.

"Not too much, how many?" Yuki asked.

"Fifty."

Yuki said something in Chinese to the other Chinese dude in the room and he grabbed the duffel bags and walked out. "I've been seein' a lot more K members than usual, what's the deal with that?"

"Hell's Angels. We're having a problem with the biker gang; it stems from a war we had with them in New York. About a week and a half ago, they caught two of our members coming out of a bar and beat them into comas. So, I pushed a memo that everyone had to travel in groups of five. And I don't care where they see a Hell's Angel at, it's on sight," Yuki's voice betrayed his frustration.

"So, you have the most rank?"

"I have the second most rant in the U.S." he confided.

"So, who's number one?" Snatch wanted to know.

"You may find out one day. Those are in your jeep by the way." He said and Snatch stood up.

"I'll be seeing you soon" Snatch walked out.

"Where are you about to go?" Alayna asked when Snatch came out of the back.

"To the hood, why, wassup?"

"I'm coming with you."

"Nah, I'm handling business right now. We can chill later on though."

"Oh, I know we goin' chill later on because you gotta come by the house. Mama was supposed to call you and tell you."

"I ain't heard from her but tell her I'll be by there tonight around eight," Snatch said while on the move.

He had too much work in his jeep to be sitting around having small talk. Snatch got in his Trackhawk and beelined it to Colony Place. He texted Action telling her it was time to get to work. Action and her mom no longer stayed in Colony Place. Action bought her mom a house in Remington and got herself a condo overlooking downtown. Snatch pulled into Holiday Park and was pleased to see that there wasn't a line of cars. He drove into Colony Place, grabbed the duffel bags and headed to Action's old apartment. Action's apartment was still where she cut the work at. Snatch tossed the duffel bags on the kitchen table and opened them up.

Once again, Yuki thought he had all the sense. Snatch had told him he only wanted fifty, but it looked like Yuki had doubled up on him again. But Snatch had been ready for it this time, he'd paid a hundred. He sent Yuki a text saying they were even because it was two point four million in the duffel bags he dropped off. Action walked in twenty minutes later looking like a meal! She had on a blue Gucci mini that showed off the fact that she had gained about twenty pounds in all the right places. Action's hair was in a Chinese bun, her lashes were done, and her toes were playing peek-a-boo in the opened-toed Gucci slingbacks she was wearing.

"Nope!" Business first" Action chided seeing the look Snatch was giving her.

"You got that" he walked over and slapped her on the ass watching it jiggle.

Action slipped out of her slingbacks and went to work. Snatch watched her work. For a few hours and left. He had to go see what him mama wanted.

"I like how you killed all that traffic" Snatch praised Tasha who was watching her workers from the hood of her H8. "Yea, the jakes were startin' to ride through a little too much" she concluded.

"You good thought?

"Good? Nigga, I'm great! I've been able to put up college funds for all five of my kids with plenty left over. I just bought a mini-mansion in the country. Nigga, life is good! But I do need to holla at you when you get a free moment," she said seriously.

"Aight. Tomorrow we'll have lunch. Say about one o'clock at Texas Roadhouse."

"I'll be there. She said and strutted off.

Snatch shook his head watching her fifty-two-inch ass. He climbed into his jeep and drove to his mom's house.

"I'm in the kitchen!"

Snatch's nose led him to the kitchen. His stomach talking shit when he walked into the kitchen. Snatch's mom had cooked fried chicken, macaroni and cheese, garlic mashed potatoes, buttermilk biscuits with gravy and string beans. Then she had a homemade apple pie in the oven.

"Dang ma, you showed out tonight." Snatch kissed her on the cheek then took a seat at the dining room table.

"I did a little something" she grinned. "Alayna come eat!" she yelled.

"Hey brookshi!" Slayna hopped in Snatch's lap.

Snatch and Alayna had a tight bond and used to always chill together but since he'd moved out, they hadn't been seeing that much of each other.

"Move so I can eat" he pushed her off of him playfully. Snatch's mom made him a big plate of food and he smashed it! The phone rang and Alayna and his mom made eye contact. His mom went to go get the phone and Snatch went and made another plate. It has been a long time since Snatch had eaten a home-cooked meal.

"Here," his mom handed him the phone

"Who is it?" He asked dipping a biscuit in the gravy

"Boy, take this phone!"

"Hello."

"What up son?" His dad's voice boomed through the phone. Quiet Storm had one of those deep, Barry White voices.

"Chillin, waiting," Snatch started playing with his food.

"I see you're a grown man now. You takin care of your responsibilities. You bought your mom a house, a Bentley, and got Alayna a Porsche. You're doing good. You're the man in the city. But I have to ask you something similar to what you asked me all those years ago. If things go wrong, are you goin' to rat?" Storm spinned it back on him.

"No. but you have to realize I was a little boy who wanted his dad and I didn't have the understanding that I do now"

"I totally understand, that's water under the bridge. Now, I've been hearin' about you and not from your mother. You know you can't do no wrong in her eyes. How long do you plan on stayin' in the game?"

Snatch weighed the question before responding. "I've never given it any thought. I'm livin' in the moment."

"You should but I'm not gonna preach to you. I do need you to tighten up though. You're on the FPD's radar. There's someone you need to meet. I set up a meetin' between y'all tomorrow at nine o'clock. They'll be at the Hilton Hotel in downtown Ralwigh in room 312. It's imperative that you attend that meetin'" Storm said.

"Aight and I got a question. Do you know someone named D-One?"

"Yeas why?" he inquired.

"He kinda calls himself takin' me under his wing. He's been givin' me the game. He owns the hottest sports bar in the city."

"Listen, that's a good nigga. Be a sponge and soak up all the game he's giving you. He's not gonna lead you astray. That old nigga is sharp" he urged.

"He said you did some real nigga shit for him back in the day." Storm chuckled. " Yea, I did," he reminisced. "I'll tell you about it one day. Is D-One still hustling?"

"I don't really know. I didn't know he hustled; to be real, I thought he just ran the bar. Pandora's is doin' numbers."

"You have sixty seconds left," the operator interrupted their convo.

"Tell your sister and mom I love them and I'll call tomorrow."

"Aight."

"Remember what I told you and stay safe. Love you son."

"Love you too" Snatch responded and hung up. Snatch finished eating and went home. His mind was scrambled trying to figure out who it was he was meeting tomorrow.

Chapter 19

Snatch woke up the next day feeling like new money! So it was only right that he looked like money. He opened his closet up and looked for something to wear. Snatch was feeling a little flashy today. He pulled a pair of white Amire shorts out and lay them across his California King. Then grabbed a blue and white Arimire button-up off the hanger and put it on the bed. He looked on the closet floor trying to decide which shoes to wear.

"Bingo," Snatch said out loud spotting a pair of white high-top Louis Vuitton sneakers.

Snatch put the outfit on and looked in the mirror and nodded his head. His drip was something out of a magazine but something was missing. Snatch went to his jewelry box and pulled out his diamond stubs, a gold Omega watch, his fronts with crushed diamonds on them and his Cuban inks. Now he was ready to op. Snatch cuffed a few bands, his clock and walked out.

It was almost one o'clock, so Snatch pushed his Trackhawk to the limit. He was doing seventy in a forty! He didn't give a fuck! He had the best lawyer in the city and his bond was already paid. Fuck twelve! He pulled into Texas Roadhouse at exactly one o'clock. Snatch strolled in and spotted Tasha in a corner booth.

"Damn, you dripping, ain't you?" she gave him a hug.

"I'm doin' a lil something," he grinned cuffing her ample backside.

"Uh un boy!" she swatted his hand away and sat back down.

"What was so important though?" Snatch asked looking over the menu.

"Snatch, first off, let me say I appreciate what you did; I'll forever be grateful but I'm almost done. Soon I'll have enough money that I won't need to hustle or work anymore for that matter. I'ma re-up two more times and that's gonna be it," she broke the news to him.

"And you're gonna have enough money to lay back?"

"More than enough but I'm going to open up some hair and nail salons. That way, I'll have a little extra comin' in but yea, I'm have plenty of bread. Snatch, I'm a multimillionaire right now but I'm sure you know that," she said.

"Okay. Well, I'm happy for you Tasha; if you ever need anything, you got my number. Now let's eat."

Snatch ordered a well-done steak and potatoes and Tash ordered a burger and fries. They ate and relaxed.

"Tasha, one day.....You gotta let me get behind that ass," he tried her.

She shook her head. Snatch, I would, but I don't need any more stalkers," she busted out laughing.

"That shit not that good."

"Hmphf! Niggas get in this tight, hot, wet gushy box and go crazy! Especially when I put my face down and arch this back" she said confidently

"You talking that talk, makin' my dick stand up."

"Maybe one day Snatch, but I seriously doubt it" Tasha dismissed him and stood up. "This bill is on you too" she walked out.

Snatch stared as her ass wobbled in the Prada jeans she had on.

"So that's what the fuck you like?" Sasha took Tasha's place.

"Where the hell you come from? You stalking me?"

"Nigga! You're fine but you ain't that damn fine. But you are looking handsome today" she complimented him.

"You're looking good too boo."

Sasha was looking like his potential wifey. Her smooth chocolate skin was moisturized and healthy-looking. Her light brown eyes had a seductive look to them. Then her lashes were on point, and her full sensuous lips had kiss me all over them. And her body wasn't like Tasha's but it was holding its own. But Snatch knew Sasha was only nineteen, so she was gonna fill out more.

"You don't looking?" Sasha questioned him as he openly admired her.

"Yea, I am, I'm ready to touch," Snatch shot back looking into her eyes.

She twisted her gloss-covered lips up. "What happened to you callin' me back? Yousa lyin' red nigga."

"Sasha, you have to know I will be havin' a lot going on. Motherfuckas be pullin' me every whicha way. Don't get it twisted, I been meanin' to but shit been hectic. Girl, I been wantin' you since that night at the club" he admitted.

"Prove it" she dared him.

"Come on," he stood up.

"Wait, I'm meeting somebody here."

"Who?"

"Mind your business."

"You are my business." Snatch was quick with his words.

"I thought you were outside." A preppy-looking white boy came up to Sasha.

"I got hungry." Sasha and the white boy swapped something in their handshake." You ready?" she asked standing up.

"What do you have goin' on?" I know a drug deal when I see one."

"You ain't the only one who hustle," Sasha smiled showing off her perfectly aligned teeth.

"Whatchu hustling?"

"Molly and pills."

That's why she stayed in the latest fashions. Snatch thought to himself. Snatch tugged on her 36-inch pink and black weave as they walked out.

"You fuck it up, you goin buy me anotha one," she threatened.

"You ain't say shit," he slapped her on the ass making her look back at him.

"Let me drop my car off so I can ride with you." Snatch followed her to her apartment where she parked and hopped in Snatch's jeep.

"So where we goin?"

"To see that new Scream movie. So what are you majoring in?"

"Early childcare and business administration. I want to open up a bunch of daycares."

"Okay, and what's up with your parents, do you have any siblings?" Snatch was feeling her out."

"My mom passed when I was ten and my dad is here but we don't be talking like that. He's too controlling and I don't have nay brothers and sisters. What about you?"

"My dad's been in prison for the last 10 years with a life sentence, my mom is here and I got a sixteen-year-old little sister that drives me crazy."

"Oh," she smiled.

They got to the movie theater in Hope Mills and he opened her door up and helped her out.

"A gentleman and a gangsta," she teased.

Snatch grabbed her hand and they walked inside. Snatch saw their reflection in the glass and he couldn't deny that they would make a good couple. While they waited in line, Snatch got behind her, wrapped his arms around her and lines his semi-hard dick up with the crack of her ass.

"You think you slick," she smiled up at him.

At 5'0 Sasha was a whole foot shorter than him. Both Sasha and Snatch were dogs when it came to the opposite sex but their chemistry was undeniable. She looked around and saw the envious looks on the faces of the women around them. Sasha was a topic of discussion in a lot of hair salons. Sasha pushed back against Snatch making him hug her tighter. Sasha had sworn off relationships, so she had to be careful because she found herself thinking of what it'd be like to be Snatch's girl.

Snatch was thinking the same thing. Sasha was wifey material. With Janice gone, there wasn't anyone to fill that void. Snatch knew Janice was most likely going to find her a college boy with a degree to settle down with because she wanted a dude that lived the legit life. Snatch could see him and Sasha getting serious. His mom's advice rang in his eyes about him finding a real rider, a girl that's all the way for him. Sasha had already checked one box. She was a rider; she'd give him Chance's addy without a second thought. And she had her own money.

They got to the window and she tried to pay for their tickets but Snatch deaded that. Then she tried to pay for their drinks, candy and popcorn but once again, Snatch said nah. She had checked another box! They got seats in the back of the theater and cozied up. Sasha was a scaredy cat! She jumped at almost every scene in the horror film. "You ain't gotta be scared, daddy got you" Snatch whispered in her ear.

She looked at him and he kissed her. Their tongues danced and Snatch's hands found her breast,

"Movie," she broke the kiss, breathless.

They watched the rest of the movie without getting frisky.

"That was actually good, where to now" asked Sasha.

"We can do whateva or go wherevea you want, I ain't got nothin' planned. Oh Shit!" Snatch looked at the time remembering he had a meeting in Raleigh at nine.

"What?'

"I gotta meet somebody in forty-five minutes. I gotta drop you off, we'll catch up tomorrow."

"Okay," she said dejectedly.

Snatch sped to her apartment, gave her a kiss and left. He pulled into the city of Raleigh thirty minutes later. Snatch found the Hilton hotel and parked. He walked in and went straight to the elevator. Snatch's designer clothes made it where the hotel staff didn't give him a second look. He got off on the third floor, proceeded to room 312 and knocked.

"Damn!" Snatch said when a woman with a bangin' body opened the door.

"Come in Sumajee and hurry up" she peeked in the hallway before closing the door. "Your ass is fine, just like your daddy. Did he tell you who and why you were meeting me?'

"Nah." Snatch admired her stacked frame.

"Good. You don't recognize who I am?" she questioned, and Snatch shook his head. "Well, me and your dad have a history, I'm Alicia by the way. I'm the police chief of Fayetteville."

Chapter 2

"The what?' Snatch had to make sure he'd heard her correctly.

"Yes I'm the police chief in Fayetteville," she said.

"What exactly is going on then? What is this meeting about?" he asked curiously.

"You and your illegal activities. I was your dad's inside scoop back in the day and now I'm going to be yours. But first, let's get my payment out of the way. I'll be expecting a quarter million dollars a month for my services." Alicia looked him square in the eyes. "Can you handle this?"

"Yea but what exactly am I getting?"

"A heads up in any investigation being done on you, the names of anyone in your circle who gets locked up and turns state, and the warning before any of your spots get raided."

This was exactly what Snatch needed to put a stronghold on the city! With her in his corner and everything else he had going for himself. CUB gang was about to be an unstoppable force. This was the last piece of the puzzle.

"I'll have the money to you tomorrow."

"Okay, I'll let you know where we'll meet at, but first, let me ask you. Is CUB gang you?" she asked, and he nodded his head." Don't leave any more calling cards in my city. That stunt hanging that boy from the red light better be your last one. Leaving your calling card eventually gets you a phone call and I can guarantee you're not gonna like who calls." She gave him some advice.

"I got my point across, so, now everyone knows the consequences of going against the grain. I can't promise you there won't be anymore examples made but I can promise that CUB gang won't be written on them. That was a special case."

"Okay, I'm going to take your work for it. And my lead detective has a hard-on for you. I've been keeping him off of you but he's still at your neck. You have to make sure you don't give him any hard evidence against you."

"What if I have someone do something to him?"

"What?!" she shrieked. "That would bring so much heat; it wouldn't be funny. Listen, I got you; everything comes through my office. First, just be smart and stop being so visual. There's no need for you to be posting up in the hood."

"I'ma do better" he grinned.

"I'll call you tomorrow and tell you where we're gonna meet" she walked towards the door.

"It's getting late, how about I just stay here tonight." Snatch wanted to fuck her thick ass. Snatch knew there wasn't a woman in the world who would be able to resist him if he could get their ear consistently.

"You can stay here tonight, just not here;" she opened the door. Snatch walked out on cloud nine. He had a lawyer, a bondsman, a police chief and a team of hustlers that were second to none. Nothing was going to stop him from ascending to the upper echelon of the underworld. And when he got there, he was going to cement his place there forever. When it was all said and done, his face was going to be on the Mount Rushmore of dope boys.

"I been in the field like children of the corn" Action rapped Future's lyrics as they sat in a mansion on the border of Cumberland County and Harnett County.

Action, Demon and Snatch all pitched in and brought a ten-bedroom, six-and-a-half bathroom, five-car garage mansion on forty acres of land. There was an indoor swimming pool, a tennis court, a twelve-seat theater, a gym, a basketball court and an arcade. The trio had designated the mansion as the Count Up mansion and the meeting spot for CUB gang.

"Y'all owe us too" Rambo spoke up.

"What are you talking about youngin?" Demon asked looking up from his phone. Me and Jason got CUB Gang across the river and Topeka Heights. My cousin Little Timmy hustles on Deep Creek Road and Sapana Road. He's trying to get on the team and Jason got a sneaky link named Jaleeya from Topeka Heights who hustles and wants to be on Count Up Bitch's"

"That's what I'm talkin' about!" Snatch said

"Oh! Hollywood Heights and the westside is ours too," Action informed them. "The crips on the westside are coppin' from us and the Holywood Heights niggas too."

"301 is also getting work from us too now," Demon added. "Most of the nigga on 301 that hustle are rockin' with us, particularly Savage. He really the man over there. And the nigga Cato from the Hill pulled up on me. He down with the gang," Demon said. "So what hood do that leave?" Snatch did a mental checklist.

"Bonnie Doane and the Murk are the only hoods left that we said we wanted and don't have," Action said.

"What up Tasha?" Snatch answered his phone. "Who are they? I'm on the way right now." Snatch hung up.

"Yo! It's the same niggas in the hood stopping the flow. They said ain't no money being made until they talk to me." Snatch rushed out the door.

"Wait for us!: They yelled.

Moggas had him fucked all the way up! They had big balls coming to his hood and making demands. Shit was about to get too bloody! Rambo and Jason hopped in the jeep with Snatch before he could pull off.

"Are we shooting first or what?" Jason checked his ARP

"I wanna see what they talking about but then, it's smoke. I can't let nothin' like this ride. It would send the city the wrong message" Snatch replied.

They pulled down into Colony Place and hopped out, pistols drawn. "Where they at?" Snatch asked Tasha.

"Right there," she pointed at two dudes with sheisty masks on posted up by a red Corvette.

Snatch, Demon and Action walked straight up to them while Rambo and Jason came around on opposite sides.

"Do you niggas have a death wish or something?" Snatch asked them.

"Nah, but our nigga wanna holla at you." The taller of the two pulled his phone out." Here he is bro," he handed Snatch the phone.

Snatch grabbed the phone and saw a light-skinned nigga with braids sitting on a couch.

"My apologies Snatch for the way I had to get your attention and my name is Milz by the way. Now that we got all the pleasantries out of the way, I'm here to tell you that you and your team are making a lot of paper in the city and me and my squad ain't a part of it" he said calmly. To get to the point, there is a drug tax in the city and I'm here to impose it. Every week, I need a light seventy-five thousand dropped at a certain----"

"Nigga, you smoking dick!" Demon cut him off

"Trust me, that ain't the route you wanna take," Milz said still calm as hell.

"You come bury ya manz" Demon blesses the two dudes with headshots.

"I thought we would've been able to handle this like adults but your man had prevented that. I'm still goin get the money but now, I'm goin get the bread and some blood" he said and ended the video call.

"Get these niggas out of here. Yo, who the fuck was doin' security?" Snatch questioned.

"Us" two dudes stepped up. "They tricked us, they acted like they wanted to buy some dope and pulled guns out." Snatch looked at Rambo and Jason because they were in charge of security and they shot both dudes in the head. "It'll never happen again."

Snatch walked off. He'd always known the jackboys were going to try their hand but he didn't expect them to try his gangsta like that. Now, he had to find out who Milz and the sheisty boys were.

Chapter 21

The next three days, there wasn't any money being made in Colony Place, Milz made sure of that. The sheisty boys were spinning through Colony Place about six times a day! They were spinning through so much that a police cruiser was posted up in the hood. Snatch was on fire! Then with them unable to get any get back was making him madder..they didn't know anything about Milz. Not where he was from, where he hung at or who he hung with for that matter. When he found out Snatch had something for him, Snatch had to take his mind off his problems, he found himself

Demon, Action, Rambo and Jason were at Pandora's. When he walked onto the third floor, NBA Youndboy's new single with Nicki Minaj was blasting. Then he saw Sasha talking to D-One. Snatch had said fuck her, he'd called her on numerous occasions and she hadn't returned any of his calls.

"I like this" Rambo grabbed the hand of one of the bottle girls.

"I bet you do" Action laughed

They got one of the elevated VIP areas and ordered five bottles of Ace of Spades. Tonight must've been game night because there was a big poker game going on, a tank game at another table, a spade tournament on a few tables and a big C-lo game.

"We goin to play Tank." Jason and Rambo went that way.

"I'm about to go take this dice game down," Demon said pulling out a knot of money.

"Hell, no boy, let's go pop this spade tournament," Action said to Snatch before he could sit down. Go ahead and get us a spot, Snatch told her watching Sasha come his way.

"Hey Snatch," Sasha smiled and he just looked at her." Ooohhh you salty! Now you see how I felt the other day when you ditched me for another bitch." She cocked her head to the side the way women do when waiting on a response to something they said.

"A bitch?" You are a simple-minded ass little girl! I ain't ditch you for no bitch, I had to handle some business! Man, get the fuck outta my face!" he tried to walk past her and she got in his way.

"I'm not the rest of these thirsty bitch's, you ain't gotta lie to me."

"Lie?"

"Bitch you got shit twisted! I don't got to lie to you. For what?! I'm that guy! It ain't nary birch I can't have. You betta open your eyes and see just who it is standing in front of you. I'm motherfuckin big boss!" Snatch snapped out.

"First off, don't call me no more bitch." She had lost some of her spunk." I apologize" she mumbled looking down at her Prada sneakers, but Snatch heard her even over the loud music.

"Prove it" he looked down at her.

Sasha looked up at him, wrapped her arms around his neck and stuck her tongue in his mouth. Snatch picked her up by her butt and she wrapped her legs around his waist. "I'm fucking you tonight." He broke the kiss and she nodded her head." "You got some of the pink molly?" Sasha reached into her bra opened a bag, put dome molly under her tongue then Snatch opened his mouth and let her put some under his tongue. Snatch put her down and walked in the direction of the spade tables with Sasha on his heels.

"There was a dive band buy in and we made the tenth team," Action stated when he woke up. Snatch took a seat across from Action and Sasha sat in his lap. They were playing with two dudes with dreds, Snatch didn't know them.

"It's best out of three. Dime first-hand equals two games, set first-hand is two games, back-to-back sets is two games. Boston anytime is three games, if you finish the game in the negatives, it's two games and if you get caught reneging, it's a game' D-one told everyone the rules.

Action got to deal first, which was a mistake on their behalf because she knew how to set the deck. Snatch and Action got a dime on the first hand eliminating the two dred heads. After the first round, there were five teams left. D-One drew names to see who would get a bye. Snatch and Action got the bye. They watched the next two games taking notes.

"Their gonna give y'all a problem" Sasha whispered in his ear.

She was referring to a team consisting of a young dude named Fred and a white dude named Spot. They were good but they were cheating. Snatch spotted that they had signs on what suits they wanted their partner to go to. Snatch wasn't worried because their overall skill wasn't up to his or Actions. He looked over to the tonic game and saw Rambo and Jason with big piles of money with them. Then he saw Demon with about a quarter mil at his feet. There was a lot of money in the building. A lot of people that had access to the third floor at Pandora's were nig money getters.

"I'm gon give you a problem tonight," Snatch whispered.

"Don't talk about it" Sasha pressed her ass against Snatch.

"Championship game is five games instead of three, but the rules stay the same," D-one said.

Snatch sat down with Sasha sitting in his lap again.

"What up Sasha?" Spot asked.

"Not shit, about to watch my nigga whoop y'all ass" she replied.

Fred got to deal first, and Action did a one-card cut. When Snatch looked at his cards, he had six spades, the ace of heart, ace of diamonds and five clubs, one of the clubs being the king. Action told Snatch she had three and a possible and Snatch went ten. Snatch pulled spades and Spot three books off the rip. Snatch was thinking that they might be hit but then Spot went to hearts giving Snatch the lead. Snatch pulled the rest of their spades, played the ace of diamond then played the eight of club. Action won with the queen and played the king of diamonds. She played the jack of diamonds; Fred played the queen of diamonds and Snatch cut it. Snatch had counted and he knew he had the last of the clubs. Snatch played the king of clubs and ran them down giving them the dime and a two-game lead.

"I told you" Sasha rubbed it in that Snatch and Action were about to win." I'll be back; I'm going to the bathroom" she got up.

"Ya'll better be winnin'" Rambo and Jason walked up with a sack full of money followed by Demon. You know me and Snatch can't be beaten in spades. How many times we don't pop y'all ass" Action bragged. Y'all talking shit but I just popped the dice game for three hundred bands" Demon bragged.

"Nigga, that's my shoe money" Rambo popped his shit. Snatch started laughing as Demon and Rambo talked shit back and forth.

"Sheisty gang! Sheisty gang!"

"Oh hell yea," Snatch looked and saw about ten dudes walking in the door pulling off their sheisty masks and Milz was in the front.

It was go time! Snatch cocked his Glock and was upping when D-One got in their way.

"No!" he said firmly.

"Man watch out," Rambo tried to step around him.

"Not in here! Be smart Snatch! You kill them in front of all these witnesses, Johnny Cochran wouldn't be able to get you off."

"Y'all chill, we goin' get 'em," Snatch said mad as hell, but D-One had a valid point.

Milz finally spotted Snatch and them. He grinned when he saw them and walked over with his crew.

"They say it's dryer than the Sahara Desert in Colony Place," he said and his niggas started laughing.

"Was it funny when you had to tell ya mons mama that her son was dead?" Demon shot back.

"And it's dry in Colony Place but you ain't stopping shit! Big bag on deck!" Action pulled out fifty bands and started making it rain on them.

"Count up!" Snatch yelled.

"Who the fuck them broke boys with get out my section!" Rambo yelled.

"Bitch, I'll beat yo ass one of the dudes stepped up.

"Whatchu waiting on?" Action dared him.

"Take that foolishness somewhere else if y'all aren't here to enjoy yourselves," D-One said.

"My bad O.G. come on let's party and leave these pussies alone," Milz said and started walking off." Oh, and tell Alayna I'll call her later on," he smiled.

"What! Rambo! Jason! Stretch 'em!" Snatch yelled.

BOC! BOC! BOC! BOC!BOC! Rambo and Jason let a barrage of bullets fly. Milz and the sheisty boys weren't no slouches because when the bullets started flying, they returned fire. Everyone who wasn't directly involved hit the ground not wanting to catch a bullet that was meant for someone else. When the shots faded, there were five sheisty boys laid out but none of them were Milz.

"This one ain't dead" Jason put his gun to his face.

"Wait! Bring him with us" said Snatch.

They were about to extract the info they needed out of him one way or the other.

Chapter 22

"Take him in there and tie him to a chair," Snatch told Demon then turned to Sasha. "I gotta take a rain check on tonight."

"No, you don't, I'm coming with you. When you're done, we're goin' to my house and you goin give me some dick" Sasha stated matter of factly, the molly already taking effect.

"Go home and I'll call you when I'm gone." Snatch didn't want her to witness what was about to go down.

"Nope. Now come on, we're wastin' time," she urged.

"Fuck it, but don't say I didn't try and warn you," he said and started off towards Actions old apartment.

When they walked in, Demon had the dude strapped to a chair.

"Damn, you're in a fucked up position! Tell me where Milz stay at and this 'll all be over," Snatch said.

"Fuck you pussy! I ain't tellin' you niggas shit" he said earning himself a punch from Snatch. "Strip him down," Snatch said.

Demon and Jason cut all his clothes off leaving him in the chair ass naked. Snatch now saw his bullet wounds. He had one in his leg and one in his side; neither looked life-threatening.

"You're goin' to tell us where Milz stay one way or the other," Demon warned him.

"Not even," he spat.

Snatch, Demon and Rambo started beating the shit out of him. When they finished, the dude's eyes were almost swollen shut and his nose looked broken.

"Now, where does he live?" Snatch asked out of breath.

"At your house"

"Hold on let me try," Sasha said as Snatch drew back to hit him again.

"Go ahead" he backed away.

"Bra, they gon' beat you to death in here and I'm not trying to see that. If you tell me when this Milz guy stay at, I can get them to let you go and this 'll all be over" Sasha said as she squatted down in front of him.

"Shorty, all that sound good," he said through swollen lips. "But y'all don't know Milz. The temporary relief that I'm getting from telling you what you want to know ain't shit compared to the agony that Milz would put not only me but my fam though.

"But I can promise you that if you give his addy up, he won't live long enough to do a thing to you," Sasha said sincerely.

"Do me a favor and kill me."

"I dint want to resort to this but you leave me no choice because I'm supposed to be getting fucked right now." She got up and walked to the kitchen. Sasha came back out with a container of salt. Sasha stuck her finger in the bullet would in his leg making him cry out.

"Aahn! You dumb bitch!"

She poured some of the salt in his bullet would and he started jerking around so much the chair tipped over. Demon and Jason fixed the chair back upright. Sasha pulled a straight razor out of her back pocket and grabbed a hold of the dude's balls. Everyone looked at her like they knew she wasn't going to cut his nuts off especially the men in the room.

"I hope that you see that I'm done playin'. I'm ready to get fucked, a bitch is horny. I'm a college girl, so I'm very intelligent and well-read. I've studied torture techniques. I also know that self-preservation is one of the strongest things known to man. So what is it goin' be, Milz or you?" she gave him the ultimatum.

"Man I ..." he paused.

Swipe! Sasha sliced his nuts off in one motion.

"aajj! Grr! Grr!" he screamed in pain.

"Oh shit!" Rambo said

All the dudes in the room grabbed their nuts. "Oh bitch, you cold-blooded vicious. Action complimented her. The dude passed out from the pain. Sasha slapped him a few times and he woke back up. The whole time, Snatch was just taking it all in, analyzing it. He made a mental note to keep his eyes on her because Sasha was showing Snatch that she had a very dark side but she was also solidifying her position as his main squeeze.

"You ready to talk?" Sasha grabbed his dick this time

"He stay in those big houses in the neighborhood right beside McDonalds by seventy-first High School. I can't remember exactly which one because he just moved over there but I do know he got a big Duke Flag and a Pittsburgh Steelers flag on each side of his front porch" he gave Milz up.

"You coulda saved yourself a lot of pain and also your life had you told them that sooner" Sasha vowed slicing his dick off and stuffing it in his mouth. Sasha put her hand over his mouth and nose causing him to choke on his own dick.

"Yooo. That nigga ate a dick" Jason said.

"She with the gang! Count up bitch's" Action stamped it.

"Now bae, I'll be outside, I'm ready to get fucked. Hurry up." Sasha said and walked out.

Boy, keep your gun cocked. That pussy right there dangerous. Demon said and everybody laughed.

"See if she got a sister!" Jason yelled as Snatch walked out.

Sasha followed Snatch to his house. She was with him the minute they walked through the door. Sasha pushed him down on the steps, wiggled out of the Balenciaga shorts she had on and straddled him.

"I want you so fucking bad!" Sasha sucked on his neck. She helped him out of his shirt and kissed her way down his body. Sasha unbuckled his Gucci belt and slid his jeans down to his ankles.

"Mmm" Sasha bit Snatches hard dick through his briefs.

"Take off that shirt," Snatch told her.

While she pulled her shirt off, Snatch took his jeans and briefs off leaving both of them naked. Sasha's chocolate body was flawless! Her D-cups sat up high and firm. Her nipples were three shades darker than her chocolate skin tone and they stood out about three inches. Snatch's eyes traveled down her body past her flat stomach down to the phat pussy. Sasha had a pair of eyes tattooed on top of her pussy. She had the words lick here on her left hip with an arrow leading to her clit. He was gonna blame it on the molly because he had the urge to taste her. Snatch hadn't ever eaten pussy before. Sasha read his mind because she closed the distance between them and walked up Snatch's body until her pussy was in his face. Sasha slowly lowered her body until her clit made contact with Snatch's mouth.

"Open your mouth daddy" she coached him, and he did as he was told.

Sasha's weight made Snatch lay all the way back on the steps.

"Ssss, that's it daddy. Suck on my clit." Sasha braced herself with her elbows on the steps looking down between her legs at Snatch as he feasted on her. "Write your name on it in cursive" she continued to coach him.

Snatch followed her instructions to a t. They locked eyes as Snatch toyed with her clit. Snatch noticed that sucking and licking on her clit made her squirm, so he kept doing it. "You gon make me cum daddy," she moaned. Snatch began to flick his tongue over Sasha's clit faster, making her rock her hips up and down.

"Asnn" Sasha gasped squirting allover Snatch's face. Snatch got from under her, leaving Sasha on her knees and elbows. Snatch lines himself up with her box and slides in.

"Uunn! Sasha tried to come up, but Snatch used his weight to push her back down.

Snatch pushed her ass up by the bottom and began to fuck Sasha with side strokes. Sasha's pussy was so wet her juices were splashing out every time he pushed in "Got damn noy!" Sasha balled her fists up as Snatch rocked her world.

The molly had both of them super horny! Sasha reached between her legs and toyed with her clit while Snatch dug her back out. Snatch pulled out and started licking her pussy from the back. He spread her ass cheeks and ran his tongue across her bootyhole.

"Oh Gawd Snatch!'

Snatch had Sasha going crazy. Snatch slid back inside her tight box and went bananas! Snatch started pounding her out hard and fast.

"Daddy! Daddy! You fucking the shit out of meee!"

"Turn over, no better yer."

Snatch stood up dick glistening with Sasha's juices. He picked Sasha up and went back inside of her. "No, no, no, no" Sasha knew Snatch was about to go in her pussy. Snatch started bouncing Sasha on his dick at a rapid pace.

"Un! Un! Un! Un!: Sasha moaned out

"Uh hud, take daddy dick!" Snatch wasn't showing Sasha no mercy. He was making a statement.

Snatch punished Sasha for two hours straight before releasing his seed inside of her.

"O.M.H." Sasha said kissing Snatch. "Are we official?"

"Yea, you my girl" Snatch made it official then he fell asleep with Sasha's head on his chest.

Chapter 23

Rambo and Jason stalked Milz's house for a week straight but he never showed his face. They decided to break in and that's when they saw it was sparely furnished. What Snatch got from that was Milz was smarter than they were giving him credit for. He didn't let his right hand know what his left hand was doing. Milz obviously only let those in his innermost circle know where he really lay his head.

"Ma, where Alayna at?" Snatch walked into his mom's house.

"In her room, why?"

Snatch didn't answer, he just walked to Alayna's room.

"You! Do you fuck with a nigga named Milz?"

"We cool but it ain't nothing serious."

"That's dead! Your not to talk to him, see him, text him or anything. Do he know where mama stay at?" Snatch was super not.

"No, and you can't tell me who I can and can't talk to" Alayna snapped.

"Alayna, I'm so serious right now. Leave him the hell alone and I'm not asking you, I'm telling you because it's some shit going on that you're unaware of."

"What is all this yelling about?" Their mom walked into the room.

"Alayna ain't trying to listen to what I'm tellin' her."

"He wants me to leave somebody alone because they don't like each other!" she folded her arms across her chest.

"Ma, this dude tried me on some extortion type of shit and now there's been bloodshed and it's only goin' to get worse. We got into it at Pandora's and he said Alayna's name. She don't understand the rules to the game."

"Aloayna, this boy can use you against your brother. Don't think that he won't. Baby, you have to realize who your brother is now and the target that he has on his back which puts one on ours as well. You see, I carry my gun all the time now. I've been through all of this before" Mia tried schooling her daughter.

"That has nothing to do with me though!"

"You sound stupid! What if he kidnaps you for ransom, than what? Huh? Stop bein so naïve Layna" Snatch said. "Fuck you Sumajee! Aint nobody tell you to go be a drug dealer! I know all about you, you forgot Ming Li is my best friend. I hope you end up in prison!" "Slap! Their mom slapped the shit out of Alayna.

"Don't you ever wish prison on him! That's your flesh and blood, he's gonna be there when nobody else is, even when these little boys are gone! All they want is some pussy! They don't fucking love you. You have thoroughbred blood in your veins! I'ma tell your father when he calls. Snatch knew that was gonna crush Alayna because she loved their dad to no end. There wasn't a bigger daddy's girl in the world than Alayna.

Snatch didn't hear the rest of what his mom said because he walked out.

"Baby, where you at?" Sasha asked when he answered his phone.

"On the way to meet Demon and Action. Whatchu doing?" "Just got done with class; about to go to the house. What do you want me to cook tonight?"

Sasha had already moved in with Snatch. They were moving fast and Snatch couldn't complain because Sasha catered to his every need. She was the perfect compliment to him."Whatever you want to be, I ain't trippin'. It's going to be a late night tonight though" he let her know.

"It better not be too late or I'm coming to find you" She warned.

"Okay baby," he chuckled.

"Bye daddy, I'll see you later on," she hung up.

Snatch pulled up to the Count Up mansion twenty minutes later.

"What up?" Snatch dapped Demon, Rambo and Jason up and hugged Action.

"Same ol, same ol. This is Rambo's cousin little Timmy and this is Jason's girl Jaleeya from Topeka Heights," said Demon.

Snatch checked them out. He didn't know why they called him little Timmy because he was about 6'2, three hundred pounds. He was dark, brown-skinned with a bald head. Snatch couldn't lie though; the big nigga was fresh as hell. He was sporting a grey Preda short set and some grey and white Prada sneakers. Little Timmy had rings on every finger and four big Cuban links around his neck. Then he turned his focus to the chick Jaleeya. She had a nice cinnamon complexion and was petite with perky B cups. She was as hell though with slanted eyes. Snatch walked to the kitchen and grabbed a bottle of Icehouse out of the refrigerator and sat down at the counter.

"I'm really not in the mood; besides, what is there for me today to them? Y'all got just as much say as I do. If y'all put them on, then that's what it is. Roll up." He was done talking about that. Alayna had Snatch feeling a certain kind of way.

"You know I know you, what's on your mind?" Action rolled up seven grams of Alien O.G. as everyone came into the kitchen. Snatch relayed it to them what happened with Alayna.

"I'm talk to sis. Your delivery was kind of wack too though" Action said as she lit the blunt.

"Man, it ain't no way!" Demon yelled into his phone."Aight,"

"What it is?" Jason asked.

"Them niggas hit two spots in Massey Hill and one of Bucks spots" demon gave them the bad news.

"How much they get?" Snatch was almost afraid to ask.

"Thirty bricks altogether"

"WOW" Action whistled because she knew that was a six-million-dollar loss.

A text came through on Snatch's phone. He looked at the text from the unknown number, it said, to think all I wanted was seventy-five bands a week, not Ima shut your whole operation down. Sheisty gang!

"When I catch this nigga Milz, he gone die in a way that's gonna make the devil cringe!" Snatch threw his beer across the kitchen.

"Are you talkin' about Sheisty gang Milz?" Jaleeya asked,

"Tell me you know that fuck nigga" Jason said.

"Do I? That's my bestie's grimy-ass baby daddy" she said.

"Tell her to come out here," Demon said, and Jaleeya called her and gave her directions to where they were.

"You do know depending on her responses it's a chance she won't leave her alive" Snatch tested her.

Jaleeya just shrugged her shoulders. This was the break they needed. The girl who walked through the door was blood-raw! She was 5'8 Puerto Rican, long brown hair down her back and thick as fuck! She put you in the mind of Jennifer Lopez.

"What up you?" Snatch asked

"Yo fine ass" She looked him up and down. She had a thick New York accent.

"Look, I need to holla at you about something and it's best that you tell me the truth," Snatch said seriously.

"Whatchu wanna know Papi? Let me guess you wanna know about Milz."

"How you know?" Rambo questioned.

"The beef between CUB gang and Sheisty gang is the talk of the city. So, what do y'all wanna know?" she popped her legs back making her ass pop out. "Everything you can tell us about him, don't leave shit out." Snatch took a deep pull on the blunt.

Milz's baby mama Mercedes told them everything there was to know about him. When she got done talking, they knew where he lived, the cars he drove, the spots he hung out at, and where his people stayed; she even told them his favorite restaurants. Milz's fun was about to end abruptly.

Chapter 24

"I got him Mike!" Detective Holt said excitedly.

"Who"

"Sumajee. Some of my informants said he runs not only Colony Place but the entire city as for the sale of heroin. He's the leader of CUB Gang which means count up boys. I also found out that he was with the entire Murk Mob and a crew of robbers called the Sheisty Boys" Detective Holt's adrenaline was rushing.

"Is this information reliable?'

"Of course, and this is coming from more than one source. Something else that I learned, you know how we've found these around every overdose in the last few months." Detective Holt held up a baggie with a baby bear on it.

"What about it?" Detective Vance didn't understand where he was going.

"What's this a picture of?"

"It looks like a small bear."

"And what is a baby bear called?" Detective Holt smiles.

"A CUB," he said and then it dawned on him." That's CUB Gang's stamp to differentiate their dope from everyone else's. "Exactly! We're going to be able to put him away forever. And he's not alone. There's Dajonte Lucas who they call Demon and Meredith Clark who goes by Action. We need to start a formal investigation. Detective Holt said as he walked in the direction of Chief Thomas' office with Detective Vance close behind.

"I've been right the whole time Chief," Detective Holt boasted.

"About what?" she looked up from the newspaper she was reading.

"Sumajee or Snatch as the street call him. I have information from reliable sources that Snatch has followed in his father's footsteps and took over our city's drug trade. He has quickly become Fayetteville's drug king"

"Are your sources willing to testify this information in front of a grand jury?" Detective Holt had Chief Thomas' undivided attention.

"Not really, I asked them that and they said to testify on him would mean a certain death."

"So what are you saying Johnathan?"

"I want permission to start a formal investigation into Snatch and CUB gang."

"Okay, but listen to me very carefully. Keep this under wraps until you have a rock-solid case because it's common knowledge that Storm had a source inside law enforcement whether in the FPD, the DA's Office or the Sheriff's Office. We never found out. But you know Storm like I do. If his source is still here and he finds out you after his firstborn and only son, I can only imagine what he will do." She let her words hang in the air

"Do you think he would have something done to a police officer?" Detective Vance questioned.

"You weren't here during Quiet Storm's reign over this city, but nothing was off limits including killing a cop. But to be fair, he wasn't overly violet but when he decided to, nobody is safe or exempt from his wrath" Detective Holt said.

"It was never proven but it was said Storm had the previous Chief of Police killed. It couldn't be proven because the body was never found" Chief Thomas informed Detective Vance. "I'll be careful," Detective Holt said and left out to get started.

When they left, Chief Thomas called Snatch and told him he needed to meet with her yesterday!

Five thirty that evening, Snatch found himself sitting in front of Chief Thomas at the Hilton again. "I don't know who they are but Detective Holt has some informants that told him all about you, your crew and who you're beefing with. It can't be anyone in your circle because they didn't give him any useful information. I think it's someone on the outside looking in. They told him stuff that's really common knowledge in the city," she told him.

"I mean as long as he ain't got no hard evidence I'm straight. And it's going be damn near impossible for that to happen because of the way I have my operation set up," Snatch said confidently.

"I okay'd him to start an investigation on y'all, so make sure your team is on their A-game because he's a real good detective. And do away with the CUB stamp. If your heroin is as good as it's supposed to be, then it will speak for itself. The less that can connect you to anything illegal, the better."

"As long as I got you on my team, I'm good regardless. I got your bread too. When I leave, unlock your doors and I'm goin' put the bag on your backseat" Snatch stood up, walked outside the Hilton, put the money in her red s550 and left.

On the way back to Fayetteville, Snatch was cruising on I95 listening to Rod Wave when about fifteen Harley Davidson's rode past. He looked and saw the back of all their jackets said Hells Angels. One had long reddish hair and a long red beard braided in one braid. Snatch called Yuki.

"What's up?" he answered on the third ring.

"Yuki what do the North Carolina chapter Hells Angels president look like?" Snatch made sure he kept up with the group.

"Real tall with long red hair and a scruffy red, braided beard. His name is Red Beard."

"Aight," Snatch hung up and called Rambo.

"What it is gang?" Rambo answered.

"Where you at?"

"Sitting in the hood with Jason bored as hell."

"Okay check it. I got some work for you but you need to hurry up. Where Action at?"

"She pulling up right now," he said getting excited.

"Good, don't let her get out. Tell her to get on the interstate and drive towards Raleigh. What she driving?"

"A blue Durango."

"Y'all hurry up!" Snatch hung up.

Snatch was about to do Yuki a solid. He followed them making sure he kept a good distance away so they didn't get spooked. Snatch knew that when you were at war, your spidey senses were heightened and you were suspicious of everything. Especially when you were at war with a deadly for like the triad.

"Boy, what the hell you got me doing?" Action called.

"All you got to do is drive and let Rambo and Jason get active. Yo! Yo! Yo! Turn around and get on this side going back towards Fayettesville. Hurry up and catch up to me in the Trackhawk." Snatch saw the blue Durango. "Put me on speakerphone."

"Go ahead," she said.

"Look, it's a group of choppas ahead of us. I want y'all to shoot all of them except the one in the front, let me worry about him. When I drive in front of them I'ma tap my brakes two times that's when u 'all let them have it," Snatch said ending the call. It was dark on the highway and there weren't that many cars out but they still had to worry about state troopers.

Snatch sped up and got in front of the motorcycles and tapped his brakes. Cha! Cha!Cha! Boc!Boc!Boc!Boc!Cha!Cha! Rambo and Jason lit the night up catching the Hells Angels by surprise. They didn't stand a chance! A few tried to speed away but Rambo and Jason mowed them down. Red beard sped up trying to get away. Snatch let him get alongside the jeep then jerked the wheel to the left hitting the bike, sending the bike skidding across the highway into the grass flipping Red Beard about ten feet in the air. Snatch pulled over and rushed to find him.

"Fuck! Fuck! Fuuuuck!" Red Beard was screaming when Snatch found him.

His left was bent at an unreal angle.

"Hey man, are you alright?" Snatch faked concern.

"Help me man, I gotta get outta here"

"Come on let me help you up."

Snatch helped Red Beard up and to his jeep sitting him in the backseat. Snatch hurried up and got back in the jeep. He pulled off while at the same time texting Yuki asking him where he was at.

Yuki: I'm at home, why?

Snatch: who???

Yuki: You have him?!!

Snatch: he's in my backseat with a broken leg

Yuki: Get him to the back on China Wok Now!

Snatch looked in the backseat and saw Red Beard had passed out. Snatch broke the speed limit getting to Fayetteville and the China Wok. When he pulled around back, Ming Li was waiting on them.

"What are you doing here?" Snatch inquired.

"Get him inside, hurry!" She looked around but didn't look worried.

Red Beard woke up as Snatch tried to move him and Snatch knocked him out with the butt of his pistol.

"In here" Ming Li directed him to the cooler where Snatch dropped him on the cold floor. "You can go now."

"I'm not leaving you here with him by yourself."

Ming Li smiled for a split second but then her face darkened.

"I not alone," she said and about ten 14K members walked in.

She kicked Red Beard in the head bringing him back to consciousness and said, "You kill my favorite uncle now you pay."

Ming Li said something in her native tongue and the 14K members lifted Red Beard up and hung him on a meat hook.

"Aahh!" he yelled.

"Hush!" Ming Li swiftly punched him in the ribs. This was totally the opposite of the sweet, goody Ming Li that Snatch was accustomed to.

Yuki walked in smiling. "You wanted to know who was first in command in the U.S. Well, you're looking at her."

"Who, Ming Li?" Snatch said in disbelief.

"Yup."

"Sumajee, you go! We talk later" Ming Li was all business as she pulled out a row of knives. Yuki escorted Snatch out to his jeep.

"She'll let you know all you need to know in due time." Snatch left thinking that he'd let pretty-ass Ming Li fool him into thinking that she was innocent and she was the real boss.

Chapter 25

"Okay, this is how it's going down, we goin' to hit all this niggas spot today. We goin' to hit this house, the two houses he's known to hang out at and we going hit his cousin's house. We gotta strike gold one time," Snatch gave Demon, Action, Rambo and Jason the rundown.

"Which one we gon' hit first?" Action questioned strapping on a lightweight vest.

"His house unless something comes up. We know he drives a red Corvette x06, a black Audi r8 gt and a white navigator on 30s. So if we spot one of them on the way, you know what it is" Snatch adjusted the strap on his vest.

"Wait, before we leave, it's somebody else coming," Rambo said.

"Who?" Snatch, Action and Demon asked at the same time.

"The newest dizzy gang member, you'll see."

" Well, they only got about five minutes and it's over," Demon said putting an extra clip in his pocket to her ar15. Someone knocked on the apartment door and Jason went to answer it. In walked a bronze-colored chick with lime green dreds that were in two braids. She was about 5'6, a hundred and sixty pounds with a baby doll face. Her features were perfect from her almond-shaped eyes, her button nose, juicy lips, the blemish-fee skin, even the shape of her face was appealing. She was a super attractive girl and she was shapely! She had some Q cups but made up for her with her hips, things and ass! Her lower half was identical to Cardi B's. It was something about her that screamed young though.

"Y'all meet India," Rambo introduced her

"Hey y'all" she squeaked out.

India had one of those low soft voices.

"You can't speak nigga?" she walked up to Demon and pushed him.

They obviously knew each other.

"What up Indy?" he said.

"Where my fucking hug, don't be tryin' to act brand new" she reached out and they hugged.

"Yo how old are you?" questioned Action reading Snatch's mind.

"Thirteen."

"Ain't no way you that young," Snatch said more to himself. "And whatchu know about a gun?"

"More than you but I can show you better than I can tell you," she answered sassily.

Snatch looked at Rambo and Jason as if to say this one is on you. They left out with Snatch, Demon and Action in his Trackhawk and Rambo, Jason and India in a dark blue Charger that she said was hers. Mil's house was in a suburban neighborhood off of Clifden Road.

"That little girl is thick as hell, I wanna her mama," Snatch said.

"Her mama phat to death too," Demon said.

"Where you know her from?" Action asked.

"I was fucking her mama a while ago but we fell out." They pulled up to Milz's house and parked. They were on some straight killa shit, so it wasn't any need for stealth. Demon did a light jog up to the door and kicked it off the hinges! Milz's house was two stories; Snatch and Action took the first floor while everyone else went upstairs. They cleared the house in two minutes with no sign of Milz.

"I found our dope!" Demon yelled from the garage.

They walked into the garage and found Demon taking bricks out of a deep freezer.

"How many is it?" Action asked

"umm....twenty five" Demon said

That meant they only took a five-brick loss. "Let's burn this bitch down," India said

"Hell yea!" Jason agreed.

"Y'all handle that " Snatch looked at the red Corvette and Navigator in the garage.

That meant Milz was driving the Audi.

"Burn them shits too" Action pointed at the cars. Action, Snatch and Demon went and got in the car while the other three got their pyromaniac on. They saw flames in the upstairs windows first then the flames appeared downstairs and the trio came running out with their arms full of shit. Snatch just shook his head. They drove off before the house was fully engulfed. The next spot they were going to was a sheisty boy hangout. They didn't know whose house it was but there were always a lot of sheisty boys there per Mercedes. The house in question was located in University Estates which coincidentally was off of the Murk. They rode past the house and saw about twenty sheisty gang dudes handing around.

"What is she doing?" Action was looking in the side mirror. Snatch looked in the rearview mirror and saw India had gotten out of her car and was walking up to the house. Snatch turned the Trackhawk around as she was approaching the group. They obviously didn't take her for a threat, their mistake. She was able to get all the way up on the group. India pulled two Glock slimline 36's out and started dumping! The shit looked like a scene out of a movie. India had both her arms outstretched, spinning in circles dropping shit. Two nigga rushed out of the front door only to join their homeboys on the highway to hell. Snatch and everybody hopped out and rushed into the house only to find it empty.

"Bitch, you sure you don't wanna be a Count Up bitch?" Action tried to snatch her up.

"Go ahead with that shit Action!" Rambo yelled.

"Nah, I ain't the hustling type. I just like spinning on shit. Ballerina life baby!" she dapped Rambo and Jason up.

"Ballerina life," Demon repeated.

"Ballerinas do a lot of spin dummy," India laughed

"Come on let's go," Snatch said.

They piled back in the cars heading to Tiffany Pines, the other sheisty gang hideout they knew about.

"Snatch, that little bitch is trained to go!" Action said excitedly.

"She a whole fool. I won't be expecting her to do all that. Rambo quietly building a crew of straight killas all employed by us," Snatch said.

"And what's crazy is all they ass is young as hell! I think the oldest is fifteen. You ain't even met all them little badass motherfuckas yet," Demon toyed with his phone.

"I can't lie that little nigga Snake creep me out though. He don't ever talk and he stay with a snake" Action shivered. Snatch hadn't met him either but he would soon. They pulled into Tiffany Pines and found the other sheisty gang handout. "If he in there, let me know but don't do nothing to him," Snatch told Rambo, Jason and India.

"Y'all not comin'?" Rambo asked.

"Y'all got it, we goin' chill."

"Why not?" Demon wanted to get active.

"That's what they're for," Snatch said watching them hit the house. "Watchin' them, particularly India, let me know we can take a step back. I mean that is why we're payin' them, right? Them motherfuckas are barely teenagers and their close to bein' millionaires; we're the bosses. I think it's about time we really started actin' like it."

"Whatchu mean?" Demon said watching the muzzle flashes going off in the house.

"Just what I said. You don't see the CEO of McDonalds takin orders and flipping burgers. We're graduated from slangin rocks to putting in work. All we need to do now is distribute the work, collect the money and give orders. It also minimizes our risk of catching a case." Snatch gave them his though process.

"I'm with that," Action agreed.

"If y'all with it, then I'm with it" Demon followed suit.

Rambo, Jason and India came out of the house shaking their heads, letting them Milz wasn't there. They had one more spot to hit before they struck out. The sun was setting as they pulled out of Tiffany Pines. They were on the way there about to pass Bonnie Doone when Action yelled "There he go!"

Snatch looked and saw Milz coming out of the J and J Fast Mart on Bragg Boulevard. Snatch swerved into the parking lot. Milz looked up, locked eyes with Snatch and upped his pistol. Boc!Boc!Boc!Boc! Milz sprayed the Trackhawk with about thirty rounds in three seconds! His gun had a switch on it. They were forced to duck down in the jeep. Snatch hopped out of the jeep with his Draco and let off as Milz was putting another clip in his gun. Cha!Cha!Cha!Cha! Snatch's bullets caused Milz to take off behind the store. Snatch chased him through the woods behind the store. Boc!Boc!Boc!Boc! Milz sprayed another clip over his shoulder making Snatch dive on the ground. Snatch got up and ran to try and catch up to Milz. Snatch came out of the woods in Field Crest Apartments and didn't see Milz anywhere. He ran down the street and saw Milz cut behind some apartments. Snatch sent some 7.62s behind him. By the time Snatch got to where he'd seen him last, he was gone. When Snatch came around the apartment with the Draco, the niggas that were posted up hustling upped their hammers. At the same time, his Trackhawk and India's charger pulled up behind him and everybody got out with big guns.

"Wassup!" Rambo screamed clutching a Russian AR47 that was bigger than him. "This rally don't what y'all wanna do," India said holding a mini14.

"Y'all ain't saying shit!" a dude said aiming a 44 bulldog. "You right, we ain't saying shit! The next few words are gonna come from this MP7," Action grilled them.

They were having a Mexican standoff.

"What the fuck goin' on?" a brown-skinned stocky dud with long dreds hopped out of a black F150 Shelbybaja Raptor.

"This nigga came out the cut clutching his Draco" a short dark-skinned dude spoke up.

Before anyone else could say a word, a white Bentley Continental pulled up and D-One got out.

"Put them guns up!" D-one yelled at the dudes and they all lowered their guns but Snatch and them kept theirs up. "Snatch you good over here, put your guns up."

They lowered their guns but kept them out.

"Now, what's the deal?" D-One asked.

"I was shootin' at this nigga Milz and he ran through here. Then when I came out of this side of the apartments lookin' for him, these niggas drew down."

"Well, all that's over now. I'm sure he is long gone by now but while you're here, there's someone you need to meet."

"Who?"

"The nigga that runs Bonnie Doone and my little brother Cricket," D-One said. "And I know this is one of the hoods that you don't have anybody in. He's your man." D-One pointed at the dude with the long dreads that had got out of the Raptor.

Chapter 26

"So, your Snatch, I've been hearing a lot about you from my brother, and your pops is a city legend," Cricket said.

"I'm sayin', so you got the whole Bonnie Doone under you?" Snatch asked as they walked away from the group.

"Under me, no, but my voice is well respected and if I can get my hands on that heroin, that y'all have, everything else will fall in line."

"Say no more, I got you" Snatch solidified his hold on the city.

Inside, Snatch was jumping for joy! CUB gang was the crème of the crop. Everyone was jumping on their bandwagon. Now it was time to weed out the bullshit and strengthen their chain. Snatch and they left Bonnie Doone and headed back to Colony Place.

"You know what bra, I think it's time for us to really let motherfucka know that we're what it is. This weekend, we're gonna round the whole gang up and go out and celebrate," Snatch said.

"It's about time! We ain't been out together since graduation night," Demon said.

"Are we goin' to a club or strip club?" questioned Jason because he'd never been to a strip club but wanted to go bad.

"Which one you wanna go to? Action inquired.

"Strip club!" Jason and Rambo both yelled, making everybody laugh.

"That's what it is then," Snatch said. "I'll call y'all and let y'all know all the details in a few days," he said and left. Snatch got in his jeep just as the phone rang.

"What up ma?" He saw ma on the screen.

"Your father is on the phone," she said.

"What up pops?"

"I talked to Alayna and got on her about her mouth. Pay her no mind. Have you taken care of the situation with this Milz boy yet?'

"Nah. He got a rabbit's foot around his neck because he dodged bullets like Neo on The Matrix but I got it under control."

"Aight, so everything else good though?"

"Hell yea! I'm surpassin' that little operation you had going on back in the day. I got the whole city riding my wave" Snatch bragged.

"Sumajee…" Storm paused. "Son, you're nowhere near my level. You are bragging about having the city, nigga, I had the whole eastern seaboard!" Storm shut down Snatch's boast. "One thing I will say is your mom said the way you assembled your team is stronger than mine's war."

"I know. Aye dad, do you remember a Detective Holt?'

"What about that coward?" Storm had a strong hatred for Detective Holt.

"He's started an investigation on me" Snatch revealed.

"Son…Do not allow him to get any evidence on you because he will try to put you where I'm at. And he's not about planting evidence either."

"Are you talking about Sabrina's husband?" Snatch's mom chimed in

"Yea," Storm answered quietly.

"Don't try and mumble it motherfucka! Snatch your punk ass Daddy was fuckin that detective's wife his dirty dick ass!" his mom snapped.

"I knew her before they were married," Storm said.

"Everybody did! That nasty ass! Murchison road ass, black ass whore. Then you had the nerve to ger her pregnant! Mia was starting to get riled up.

"She had an abortion, Mia!" Storm's voice boomed. Snatch hung up because his dad yelling back was about to set his mom off. Snatch was still sitting in Colony Place, he hadn't pulled off because the convo with his dad had grabbed his attention. He cranked the jeep up as Action tapped on his window.

"What up?" He unlocked the door.

"You tryin' to hit this? It's some shit called weddin' cake" she passed him the blunt.

"Where the hell you be getting all this exclusive ass weed from?" Snatch hit the blunt and started coughing.

This Jamaican nigga named King. He stays with that fire, he ain't never got no trash," she said as she blew smoke circles.

"I want a pound of that and make sure the whole gang knows about us celebration on Saturday night. We gon do it at Pleasure's Paradise."

"Okay, I want some dick," she reached out and grabbed Snatch's dick.

"Tomorrow boo.'

"Aight" she got out of the jeep leaving him the blunt. Snatch sat in the jeep smoking and thinking to himself. His dad's words were ringing in his ears about him having the whole East coast. The more Snatch thought about it, the more he didn't see why he couldn't surpass that and take over the U.S. period. That led his thoughts to Ming Li. The whole time, she had been the one calling the shots. Snatch had yet to talk to her since the night he'd taken Red Beard to the China Wok. Snatch was going to tell her about herself the next time he saw her. Demon came out of the apartment with India following behind him. They both got in Demons Escalade and rode off.

"I know he not about to fuck that little girl," Snatch said out loud, shaking his head and drove home.

"Oh my God, baby!" Sasha squeaked as Snatch put a diamond necklace around her neck.

"You are silly, can I get dressed now?" It was Saturday night and he had to get ready for the CUB Gang celebration at Pleasure's Paradise. He'd already secured VIP areas and passes. It was already nine-thirty, so he was already gonna be late. Snatch grabbed the outfit Sasha had laid out for him. Sasha had gotten them matching Prada outfits. Sasha had gotten him a pair of black Prada shorts, a purple Pradabutton-up and some black and purple Jordan fours. Sasha was wearing some black Prada skinny jeans that looked like someone had drawn them on her, a purple Prada halter and some black six-inch stilettos. Snatch put his outfit on and checked himself out. He couldn't front Sasha, she had done her thing; he was looking good as hell but he was about to put the finishing touches on it. Done was the low-key style he was putting on. He had bought Audemars Piquet watch and had it busted down with yellow vv5s costing him three hundred and fifty thousand dollars.

Then he brought two new Cuban links and had yellow vv5s in them as well. Snatch had gold rings on every finger including his thumbs. He'd also put a quarter mil in his grill. He had eight on top and eight on bottom with yellow and blue diamonds in them. Snatch had gone all out on Sasha's jewelry game as well. He'd gotten her yellow diamond necklace, a yellow diamond tennis bracelet, a presidential Rolex busted down in yellow diamonds. Then he'd gotten her a grill made but only for her bottom four, it was also yellow diamonds.

"Come here Daddy," Sasha called him over to the full-length mirror.

She positioned herself in front of him and snapped a selfie.

"I'm posting this on the book and Instagram," she smiled.

"Let's go!" Snatch put on a few dabs of Issey Miyccke and walked downstairs to the garage. Snatch could only smile as he looked at his brand new 2023 Volcano yellow over black Lamborghini Aventador. Snatch wasn't playing any games, he was big boy stunting tonight. He put his Gucci duffel bag in the trunk and got in.

"Damn bae, you was goin' leave me?" she smiles, her grill gleaming.

"You beautiful baby," he praised her

"Thank you Daddy" she kissed him on the lips.

They pulled up to the strip club and Snatch parked in front of the building.

"Aint No way" Sasha looked at the parking lot through the tint.

"What?"

"All of them are CUB gang?" she asked

There were at least two hundred people chilling in the parking lot. There were so many foreigners, it looked like a car show. Snatch got out the Lambo and everybody rushed him.

"Yea nigga! We deep as a bitch!" Demon yelled dapping him up. Demon was wearing that shit. He was Amiri down.

"Hands down, this is our city" Action hugged him looking fine as hell in a gold Ferragamo body suit.

"Dizzy gang!" Rambo yelled and thirty other people yelled Dizzy gang.

Snatch looked at everyone who had yelled Dizzy gang and the first thing he noticed was that all of them were wearing some kind of Dolce and Gabbana. The next thing he noticed was that all of them are young!. The oldest kid migh've been fifteen."

"Why all y'all got on Dolce?" Snatch wanted to know.

"That's our symbol, DG means Dizzy gang," Jason told him.

"I like that" Snatch grinned.

All the main CUB gang members were in attendance. Snatch saw Little Timmy, Jaleeya, Savage, Cato, Cricket, Ray Nate, Trigga Tone, Ak, Lil Buck, Tasha, Zay and Los. Snatch smiled on the inside; his squad was comprised of top-notch hustlers! Snatch looked at the newest members. Both Trigga and Ak were 5'7, brown-skinned, with long dreds and tatted up. They ran Ramsey Street with an iron fist. Ray Nate was 6'0 light skinned brush cut and had a stocky build. He had Shaw Road doing numbers. He was muscular as hell with shoulder-length dreds. Downtown was booming because of him. Savage had 301 on Smash! Savage was dark brown skinned with real long dreds and was Snoop Dog skinny and got super active. He stayed with a coppa.

They filed in the club and spread out. The strippers went crazy when they walked in. Snatch walked up to the main stage, pulled out thirty bands out of a Gucci duffel and tossed it on stage. Snatch walked up to the VIP section and grabbed a seat with Sasha in his lap.

"I'm goin' grab me a stripper. I'll check y'all out later," Demon said and walked down the steps.

Everyone left VIP leaving Sasha and Snatch alone. Snatch went in the duffel, pulled out fifty bands and told the bottle girl "I'm trying to buy the bar, bring me a bottle of Peach Circo. And keep whatever is left."

Snatch walked to the edge of VIP area and started throwing bands in the air. He didn't bother to trade for no one. Snatch was throwing fifties and hundreds. He got the bottle from the bottle girl and turned it up. "You want some baby?" Snatch asked Sasha.

"I don't know if I can drink yet."

"What the hell does that mean?" He questioned throwing money on a thick red bone that was making her ass clap.

"See, I wasn't gonna tell you until I knew for sure but I think I'm pregnant. I got a doctor's appointment tomorrow to find out for sure." Sasha looked at him to judge his reaction.

"What?!" he picked her up and kissed her. "I'ma be a daddy!" Snatch beamed.

"I don't know yet, I took a home pregnancy test and it said I was. I wanna see what the doctor says."

"I'm going with you," he said slapping her on the butt.

They shared a kiss and went to throwing money. There was so much money throughout the club on the floor that you couldn't even see the carpet! CUB and Dizzy gang were making a statement.

"Y'all need to come get Demon!" India ran into the VIP section.

Snatch looked out over the crowd and saw Demon with his hand in the face of a bouncer. Snatch rushed down the steps to where the altercation was.

"Man, what the fuck is going on?" Snatch asked.

"This hat-in-ass nigga mad because I grabbed a bottle girl ass. Shit, she ain't complaining. This nigga better get his shit together before it get bloody." Demon threatened clearly on the way to being drunk.

"You get out since you threatening me," the bouncer said.

"Look bro, it ain't even that serious, he good" Snatch tried to de-escalate the situation.

"Nah, he gotta go."

Snatch looked around and saw the Dizzy gang members licking their chops.

"I ain't going nowhere nigga!" Demon said still in the bouncer's face.

The bouncer made the mistake of trying to grab Demon; everything went to hell! Before the bouncer could grab Demon, Rambo and Dizzy gang converged on him. The bouncer hit the ground and there were so many feet on him that you would have thought he was a human soccer ball. Snatch pulled Sasha out of the commotion. The other bouncers started spraying mace in the crowd making everyone rush them. Snatch rushed Sasha out of the club and to the Lambo.

"Go home, I'll be there in a minute." He rushed back inside the club to break the melee up.

When Snatch walked back into the club, his gang was stomping the bouncers out.

"Y'all come on!" he screamed and they rushed out.

Snatch could tell Demon was on the verge of being drunk, so he took his keys and got in the driver's seat of his McLaren 600lt coupe.

"I'm taking Demon home, y'all don't get in no more shit," Snatch told his gang out the window and pulled off.

Snatch drove Demon home which was on the other side of town in a gated community called Country Club Estates.

"Snatch, something doesn't seem right," Demon said glancing around. They had just pulled up to Demon's house and Snatch was about to drop him off and he is going to head home; tomorrow was going to be a big day.

"What is it brody?" Snatch questioned reaching for his stick.

"I don't know, something just seems kinda off" Demon cocked his XD.40 and got out. Snatch got out with Demon, his pistol down by his side. The full moon was giving off just enough light that the night wasn't pitch black.

Snatch now felt what Demon was feeling. Everything was eerily quiet; the crickets weren't even chirping. Snatch shivered and got goosebumps. Snatch and Demon looked around one last time before entering the house. Demon cut the lights on in the house and they went through the house room by room making sure everything was to the good and nobody was in hiding.

"Yous'a scary ass, pussy ass nigga" Snatch pushed Demon. "Something doesn't seem right" he mocked Demon.

"Whateva motherfucka. You better take your ass home before the wifey do something to your ass. You know you're supposed to be home before streetlights come on, Demon gave it back. "What? Nigga, I'm the king of my castle," Snatch bragged opening the door.

Whap! Whap! Something hard hit Snatch twice in the face causing him to stumble backwards into Demon. Demon caught Snatch and they both fell to the carpet.

"Surprise! You motherfuckers thought that shit was sweet but now it's time to pay the piper. Well, Snatch, you're going to pay the piper, but you Mr. Demon, you're about to pay the devil a visit," he pointed his gun at Demon and squeezed the trigger. Boom! Boom! Boom! "Now you have to bury your mans."

Lock Down Publications and Ca$h Presents Assisted Publishing Packages

BASIC PACKAGE $499 Editing Cover Design Formatting	UPGRADED PACKAGE $800 Typing Editing Cover Design Formatting
ADVANCE PACKAGE $1,200 Typing Editing Cover Design Formatting Copyright registration Proofreading Upload book to Amazon	LDP SUPREME PACKAGE $1,500 Typing Editing Cover Design Formatting Copyright registration Proofreading Set up Amazon account Upload book to Amazon Advertise on LDP, Amazon and Facebook Page

***Other services available upon request.
Additional charges may apply

Lock Down Publications
P.O. Box 944
Stockbridge, GA 30281-9998
Phone: 470 303-9761

Submission Guideline

Submit the first three chapters of your completed manuscript to ldpsubmissions@gmail.com. In the subject line add **Your Book's Title**. The manuscript must be in a Word Doc file and sent as an attachment. Document should be in Times New Roman, double spaced, and in size 12 font. Also, provide your synopsis and full contact information. If sending multiple submissions, they must each be in a separate email.

Have a story but no way to send it electronically? You can still submit to LDP/Ca$h Presents. Send in the first three chapters, written or typed, of your completed manuscript to:

LDP: Submissions Dept
P.O. Box 944
Stockbridge, GA 30281-9998

DO NOT send original manuscript. Must be a duplicate.
Provide your synopsis and a cover letter containing your full contact information.

Thanks for considering LDP and Ca$h Presents.

NEW RELEASES

BLOODLINE OF A SAVAGE 1&2
THESE VICIOUS STREETS 1&2
RELENTLESS GOON
RELENTLESS GOON 2
BY PRINCE A. TAUHID

THE BUTTERFLY MAFIA 1-3
BY FUMIYA PAYNE

A THUG'S STREET PRINCESS 1&2
BY MEESHA

CITY OF SMOKE 2
BY MOLOTTI

STEPPERS 1,2&3
THE REAL BADDIES OF CHI-RAQ
BY KING RIO

THE LANE 1&2
BY KEN-KEN SPENCE

THUG OF SPADES 1&2
LOVE IN THE TRENCHES 2
CORNER BOYS
BY COREY ROBINSON

TIL DEATH 3
BY ARYANNA

THE BIRTH OF A GANGSTER 4
BY DELMONT PLAYER

PRODUCT OF THE STREETS 1&2
BY DEMOND "MONEY" ANDERSON

NO TIME FOR ERROR
BY KEESE

MONEY HUNGRY DEMONS
BY TRANAY ADAMS

Coming Soon from Lock Down Publications/Ca$h Presents

IF YOU CROSS ME ONCE 6
ANGEL V
By Anthony Fields

IMMA DIE BOUT MINE 5
By Aryanna

A THUGS STREET PRINCESS 3
By Meesha

PRODUCT OF THE STREETS 3
By Demond Money Anderson

CORNER BOYS 2
By Corey Robinson

THE MURDER QUEENS 6&7
By Michael Gallon

CITY OF SMOKE 3
By Molotti

CONFESSIONS OF A DOPE BOY
By Nicholas Lock

THA TAKEOVER
By Keith Chandler

BETRAYAL OF A G 2
By Ray Vinci

CRIME BOSS
By Playa Ray

Available Now

RESTRAINING ORDER 1 & 2
By **CA$H & Coffee**

LOVE KNOWS NO BOUNDARIES 1-3
By **Coffee**

RAISED AS A GOON I, II, III & IV
BRED BY THE SLUMS I, II, III
BLAST FOR ME I & II
ROTTEN TO THE CORE I II III
A BRONX TALE I, II, III
DUFFLE BAG CARTEL I II III IV V VI
HEARTLESS GOON I II III IV V
A SAVAGE DOPEBOY I II
DRUG LORDS I II III
CUTTHROAT MAFIA I II
KING OF THE TRENCHES
By **Ghost**

LAY IT DOWN I & II
LAST OF A DYING BREED I II
BLOOD STAINS OF A SHOTTA I & II III
By **Jamaica**

LOYAL TO THE GAME I II III
LIFE OF SIN I, II III
By **TJ & Jelissa**

IF LOVING HIM IS WRONG…I & II
LOVE ME EVEN WHEN IT HURTS I II III
By **Jelissa**

PUSH IT TO THE LIMIT
By **Bre' Hayes**

BLOODY COMMAS I & II
SKI MASK CARTEL I, II & III
KING OF NEW YORK I II, III IV V
RISE TO POWER I II III
COKE KINGS I II III IV V
BORN HEARTLESS I II III IV
KING OF THE TRAP I II
By **T.J. Edwards**

WHEN THE STREETS CLAP BACK I & II III
THE HEART OF A SAVAGE I II III IV
MONEY MAFIA I II
LOYAL TO THE SOIL I II III
By **Jibril Williams**

A DISTINGUISHED THUG STOLE MY HEART I II & III
LOVE SHOULDN'T HURT I II III IV
RENEGADE BOYS 1-4
PAID IN KARMA 1-3
SAVAGE STORMS 1-3
AN UNFORESEEN LOVE 1-3
BABY, I'M WINTERTIME COLD 1-3
A THUG'S STREET PRINCESS 1&2
By **Meesha**

A GANGSTER'S CODE 1-3
A GANGSTER'S SYN 1-3
THE SAVAGE LIFE 1-3
CHAINED TO THE STREETS 1-3
BLOOD ON THE MONEY 1-3
A GANGSTA'S PAIN 1-3
BEAUTIFUL LIES AND UGLY TRUTHS
CHURCH IN THESE STREETS
By **J-Blunt**

CUM FOR ME 1-8
An LDP Erotica Collaboration

BLOOD OF A BOSS 1-5
SHADOWS OF THE GAME
TRAP BASTARD
By **Askari**

THE STREETS BLEED MURDER 1-3
THE HEART OF A GANGSTA 1-3
By **Jerry Jackson**

WHEN A GOOD GIRL GOES BAD
By **Adrienne**

THE COST OF LOYALTY 1-3
By **Kweli**

BRIDE OF A HUSTLA 1-3
THE FETTI GIRLS 1-3
CORRUPTED BY A GANGSTA 1-4
BLINDED BY HIS LOVE
THE PRICE YOU PAY FOR LOVE 1-3
DOPE GIRL MAGIC 1-3
By **Destiny Skai**

A KINGPIN'S AMBITION
A KINGPIN'S AMBITION II
I MURDER FOR THE DOUGH
By **Ambitious**

TRUE SAVAGE 1-7
DOPE BOY MAGIC 1-3
MIDNIGHT CARTEL 1-3
CITY OF KINGZ 1&2
NIGHTMARE ON SILENT AVE
THE PLUG OF LIL MEXICO 1&2
CLASSIC CITY
By **Chris Green**

CONFESSIONS OF A DOPEBOY | NICHOLAS LOCK

A GANGSTER'S REVENGE 1-4
THE BOSS MAN'S DAUGHTERS 1-5
A SAVAGE LOVE 1&2
BAE BELONGS TO ME 1&2
A HUSTLER'S DECEIT 1-3
WHAT BAD BITCHES DO 1-3
SOUL OF A MONSTER 1-3
KILL ZONE
A DOPE BOY'S QUEEN 1-3
TIL DEATH 1-3
IMMA DIE BOUT MINE 1-4
By **Aryanna**

A DOPEBOY'S PRAYER
By **Eddie "Wolf" Lee**

THE KING CARTEL 1-3
By **Frank Gresham**

THESE NIGGAS AIN'T LOYAL 1-3
By **Nikki Tee**

GANGSTA SHYT 1-3
By **CATO**

THE ULTIMATE BETRAYAL
By **Phoenix**

BOSS'N UP 1-3
By **Royal Nicole**

I LOVE YOU TO DEATH
By **Destiny J**

I RIDE FOR MY HITTA
I STILL RIDE FOR MY HITTA
By **Misty Holt**

LOVE & CHASIN' PAPER
By **Qay Crockett**

TO DIE IN VAIN
SINS OF A HUSTLA
By **ASAD**

BROOKLYN HUSTLAZ
By **Boogsy Morina**

BROOKLYN ON LOCK 1 & 2
By **Sonovia**

GANGSTA CITY
By **Teddy Duke**

A DRUG KING AND HIS DIAMOND 1-3
A DOPEMAN'S RICHES
HER MAN, MINE'S TOO 1&2
CASH MONEY HO'S
THE WIFEY I USED TO BE 1&2
PRETTY GIRLS DO NASTY THINGS
By **Nicole Goosby**

LIPSTICK KILLAH 1-3
CRIME OF PASSION 1-3
FRIEND OR FOE 1-3
By **Mimi**

TRAPHOUSE KING 1-3
KINGPIN KILLAZ 1-3
STREET KINGS 1&2
PAID IN BLOOD 1&2
CARTEL KILLAZ 1-3
DOPE GODS 1&2
By **Hood Rich**

THE STREETS ARE CALLING
By **Duquie Wilson**

STEADY MOBBN' 1-3
THE STREETS STAINED MY SOUL 1-3
By **Marcellus Allen**

WHO SHOT YA 1-3
SON OF A DOPE FIEND 1-4
HEAVEN GOT A GHETTO 1&2
SKI MASK MONEY 1&2
By **Renta**

GORILLAZ IN THE BAY 1-4
TEARS OF A GANGSTA 1/&2
3X KRAZY 1&2
STRAIGHT BEAST MODE 1&2
By **DE'KARI**

TRIGGADALE 1-3
MURDA WAS THE CASE 1-3
By **Elijah R. Freeman**

SLAUGHTER GANG 1-3
RUTHLESS HEART 1-3
By **Willie Slaughter**

GOD BLESS THE TRAPPERS 1-3
THESE SCANDALOUS STREETS 1-3
FEAR MY GANGSTA 1-5
THESE STREETS DON'T LOVE NOBODY 1-2
BURY ME A G 1-5
A GANGSTA'S EMPIRE 1-4
THE DOPEMAN'S BODYGAURD 1&2
THE REALEST KILLAZ 1-3
THE LAST OF THE OGS 1-3
By **Tranay Adams**

MARRIED TO A BOSS 1-3
By **Destiny Skai & Chris Green**

KINGZ OF THE GAME 1-7
CRIME BOSS 1-3
By **Playa Ray**

FUK SHYT
By **Blakk Diamond**

DON'T F#CK WITH MY HEART 1&2
By **Linnea**

ADDICTED TO THE DRAMA 1-3
IN THE ARM OF HIS BOSS
By **Jamila**

LOYALTY AIN'T PROMISED 1&2
By **Keith Williams**

YAYO 1-4
A SHOOTER'S AMBITION 1&2
BRED IN THE GAME
By **S. Allen**

TRAP GOD 1-3
RICH $AVAGE 1-3
MONEY IN THE GRAVE 1-3
CARTEL MONEY
By **Martell Troublesome Bolden**

FOREVER GANGSTA 1&2
GLOCKS ON SATIN SHEETS 1&2
By **Adrian Dulan**

TOE TAGZ 1-4
LEVELS TO THIS SHYT 1&2
IT'S JUST ME AND YOU
By **Ah'Million**

CONFESSIONS OF A DOPEBOY | NICHOLAS LOCK

KINGPIN DREAMS 1-3
RAN OFF ON DA PLUG
By **Paper Boi Rari**

THE STREETS MADE ME 1-3
By **Larry D. Wright**

CONFESSIONS OF A GANGSTA 1-4
CONFESSIONS OF A JACKBOY 1-3
CONFESSIONS OF A HITMAN
By **Nicholas Lock**

I'M NOTHING WITHOUT HIS LOVE
SINS OF A THUG
TO THE THUG I LOVED BEFORE
A GANGSTA SAVED XMAS
IN A HUSTLER I TRUST
By **Monet Dragun**

QUIET MONEY 1-3
THUG LIFE 1-3
EXTENDED CLIP 1&2
A GANGSTA'S PARADISE
By **Trai'Quan**

CAUGHT UP IN THE LIFE 1-3
THE STREETS NEVER LET GO 1-3
By **Robert Baptiste**

NEW TO THE GAME 1-3
MONEY, MURDER & MEMORIES 1-3
By **Malik D. Rice**

CREAM 2-3
THE STREETS WILL TALK
By **Yolanda Moore**

THE STREETS WILL NEVER CLOSE 1-3
By **K'ajji**

LIFE OF A SAVAGE 1-4
A GANGSTA'S QUR'AN 1-4
MURDA SEASON 1-3
GANGLAND CARTEL 1-3
CHI'RAQ GANGSTAS 1-4
KILLERS ON ELM STREET 1-3
JACK BOYZ N DA BRONX 1-3
A DOPEBOY'S DREAM 1-3
JACK BOYS VS DOPE BOYS 1-3
COKE GIRLZ
COKE BOYS
SOSA GANG 1&2
BRONX SAVAGES
BODYMORE KINGPINS
BLOOD OF A GOON
By **Romell Tukes**

CONCRETE KILLA 1-3
VICIOUS LOYALTY 1-3
By **Kingpen**

THE ULTIMATE SACRIFICE 1-6
KHADIFI
IF YOU CROSS ME ONCE 1-3
ANGEL 1-4
IN THE BLINK OF AN EYE
By **Anthony Fields**

THE LIFE OF A HOOD STAR
By **Ca$h & Rashia Wilson**

NIGHTMARES OF A HUSTLA 1-3
BLOOD AND GAMES 1&2
By **King Dream**

GHOST MOB
By **Stilloan Robinson**

HARD AND RUTHLESS 1&2
MOB TOWN 251
THE BILLIONAIRE BENTLEYS 1-3
REAL G'S MOVE IN SILENCE
By **Von Diesel**

MOB TIES 1-7
SOUL OF A HUSTLER, HEART OF A KILLER 1-3
GORILLAZ IN THE TRENCHES
By **SayNoMore**

BODYMORE MURDERLAND 1-3
THE BIRTH OF A GANGSTER 1-4
By **Delmont Player**

FOR THE LOVE OF A BOSS 1&2
By **C. D. Blue**

KILLA KOUNTY 1-5
By **Khufu**

MOBBED UP 1-4
THE BRICK MAN 1-5
THE COCAINE PRINCESS 1-10
STEPPERS 1-3
SUPER GREMLIN 1-4
By **King Rio**

MONEY GAME 1&2
By **Smoove Dolla**

A GANGSTA'S KARMA 1-4
By **FLAME**

KING OF THE TRENCHES 1-3
By **GHOST & TRANAY ADAMS**

CONFESSIONS OF A DOPEBOY | NICHOLAS LOCK

QUEEN OF THE ZOO 1&2
By **Black Migo**

GRIMEY WAYS 1-3
BETRAYAL OF A G
By **Ray Vinci**

XMAS WITH AN ATL SHOOTER
By **Ca$h & Destiny Skai**

KING KILLA 1&2
By **Vincent "Vitto" Holloway**

BETRAYAL OF A THUG 1&2
By **Fre$h**

THE MURDER QUEENS 1-5
By **Michael Gallon**

FOR THE LOVE OF BLOOD 1-4
By **Jamel Mitchell**

HOOD CONSIGLIERE 1&2
NO TIME FOR ERROR
By **Keese**

PROTÉGÉ OF A LEGEND 1&2
LOVE IN THE TRENCHES 1&2
By **Corey Robinson**

THE PLUG'S RUTHLESS DAUGHTER
By **Tony Daniels**

BORN IN THE GRAVE 1-3
CRIME PAYS
By **Self Made Tay**

MOAN IN MY MOUTH
By **XTASY**

CONFESSIONS OF A DOPEBOY | NICHOLAS LOCK

TORN BETWEEN A GANGSTER AND A GENTLEMAN
By **J-BLUNT & Miss Kim**

LOYALTY IS EVERYTHING 1-3
CITY OF SMOKE 1&2
By **Molotti**

HERE TODAY GONE TOMORROW 1&2
By **Fly Rock**

WOMEN LIE MEN LIE 1-4
FIFTY SHADES OF SNOW 1-3
STACK BEFORE YOU SPLURGE
GIRLS FALL LIKE DOMINOES
NAÏVE TO THE STREETS
By **ROY MILLIGAN**

PILLOW PRINCESS
By **S. Hawkins**

THE BUTTERFLY MAFIA 1-3
SALUTE MY SAVAGERY 1&2
By **Fumiya Payne**

THE LANE 1&2
By Ken-Ken Spence

THE PUSSY TRAP 1-5
By **Nene Capri**

DIRTY DNA
By **Blaque**

SANCTIFIED AND HORNY
by **XTASY**

BOOKS BY LDP'S CEO, CA$H

TRUST IN NO MAN
TRUST IN NO MAN 2
TRUST IN NO MAN 3
BONDED BY BLOOD
SHORTY GOT A THUG
THUGS CRY
THUGS CRY 2
THUGS CRY 3
TRUST NO BITCH
TRUST NO BITCH 2
TRUST NO BITCH 3
TIL MY CASKET DROPS
RESTRAINING ORDER
RESTRAINING ORDER 2
IN LOVE WITH A CONVICT
LIFE OF A HOOD STAR
XMAS WITH AN ATL SHOOTER

www.ingramcontent.com/pod-product-compliance
Lightning Source LLC
LaVergne TN
LVHW020543140225
803645LV00001B/149